Praise for *The Revealers*

This is a story that reveals how hard middle school can really be. It makes you think twice about what you might be doing to hurt other people. Believe the unbelievable . . . and let Russell, Catalina, and Elliot reveal the truth.

—Kate, age 12 / Norwich, Vermont

This is an inspiring book about sticking up for yourself, and being brave. I believe every kid should read this book.

—Emily, age 12 / Jericho, Vermont

Fun, truthful, and realistic.

—Christina, age 13 / Danvers, Massachusetts

It was quite an experience reading this book to my homeroom reading group. There were kids speaking out who I would not have guessed would be willing to share their experiences. *The Revealers* touched a nerve.

—Mary Lou Massucco, teacher / Bellows Falls, Vermont

When my class read *The Revealers*, it was very addictive and I finished early. Now I'm reading it to my 18-year-old sister and my mom, and they are begging for more.

—Brian, age 12 / San Jose, California

This story about school bullies made me think about why kids are so mean to each other. It inspired me to step out of my clique and meet new friends, and help people who may be bullied.

—David Lackner, age 11 / "The Book That Changed Me,"
The Washington Post Book World

Every page and chapter rings true with the angst, isolation, drama, confusion, and humor of middle school kids trying to find their way through the cruel and complex social order of early puberty.

—Patricia S. Worsham, National Board Certified Teacher
and English Department chair / Lynchburg, Virginia

This book taught me how to cope with bullying. It actually really helped me. I had been having trouble fitting in and *The Revealers* allowed me to see that it was okay to be myself.

—Hannah, age 12 / Greenwood, Maine

This is one of the best books in a long time for getting kids to read. It's even better for getting them to write.

—Karon Perron, teacher and parent / Castleton, Vermont

My teenage daughter and I highly recommend this book, not only for middle school students but for parents and teachers. My advice, after you read it: pass it on and share your feelings and thoughts with others!

—Becky Carlson, coordinator, Sussex County Coalition
for Healthy and Safe Families / Newton, New Jersey

THE
REVEALERS

Also by Doug Wilhelm

Raising the Shades

Falling

Choose Your Own Adventure Books

The Forgotten Planet

Scene of the Crime

The Secret of Mystery Hill

Search the Amazon!

Gunfire at Gettysburg

Shadow of the Swastika

The Gold Medal Secret

The Underground Railroad

THE REVEALERS

DOUG WILHELM

SQUARE
FISH

FARRAR STRAUS GIROUX

NEW YORK

SQUARE
FISH

An Imprint of Macmillan

THE REVEALERS. Copyright © 2003 by Doug Wilhelm.
All rights reserved. Printed in the United States of America by
R. R. Donnelley & Sons Company, Harrisonburg, Virginia. For information, address
Square Fish, 175 Fifth Avenue, New York, NY 10010.

Square Fish and the Square Fish logo are trademarks of Macmillan and
are used by Farrar Straus Giroux under license from Macmillan.

Library of Congress Cataloging-in-Publication Data
Wilhelm, Doug.
The revealers / Doug Wilhelm.
p. cm.
Summary: Tired of being bullied and picked on, three seventh-grade outcasts join
forces and, using scientific methods and the power of a local area network (LAN),
begin to create a new atmosphere at Parkland Middle School.
ISBN 978-0-312-56374-5
[1. Bullies—Fiction.   2. Internet—Fiction.   3. Friendship—Fiction.
4. Schools—Fiction.]   I. Title.

PZ7.W648145 Re 2003
[Fic]—dc21

2002035321

Excerpts from *Anne Frank: The Diary of a Young Girl* by Anne Frank, translated
by B. M. Mooyaart-Doubleday, copyright © 1952 by Otto H. Frank, used by
permission of Doubleday, a division of Random House, Inc.

Originally published in the United States by Farrar Straus Giroux
First Square Fish Edition: September 2011
Square Fish logo designed by Filomena Tuosto
mackids.com

5   7   9   10   8   6   4

AR: 3.7 / LEXILE: 580L

We are all islands
till comes the day
we cross the burning water
Johnny Clegg,
South African songwriter

For Sarah-Lee

CONTENTS

THE
REVEALERS

RICHIE

When I was in seventh grade I did not understand the things that came out of my mouth. Of course I'm a year older now, and a *lot* happened last year—and that's what this story is about—but sometimes I think back and I just cringe.

I wanted people to say, "Hey, Russell! Sit with us!" But I'd open my mouth and what would come out would be loud and clanky and wrong. And they would give me that quick, flat, puzzled stare that is the stock weapon of the cool seventh grader and seems to ask, "What species are you, exactly?" And I would go away thinking I was hopeless. I just wished that once I could say the right thing—but next chance I had with somebody important my words would pop out clanky and loud and I would want to run my head into a wall. I'd wonder, What *happened* to me?

Basically, when seventh grade started I found out I was out. It was like everyone else took a secret summer course in how to act, what to say, and what groups to be in, and I never found out about it. Maybe they didn't tell me on purpose. Maybe they thought it'd be fun to see how out of it I could get. See how you could start to think? But the truth is, nobody thought about me much at all back then. I wasn't the type anybody paid attention to—not before all this started happening.

So I would go home from school by myself. I was riding my bike the particular day when this thing occurred that pretty much captures what I'm talking about: my having had this talent, just then in my life, for saying an incredibly wrong thing to exactly the person I should never, ever have said it to.

I was taking my time, that afternoon. I had nowhere special to go. My mom doesn't get home till about five-thirty, later if she has to go to the store. And I liked to dawdle along. I mean, after a whole day of being herded—having to go here, sit there, and rush with the crowds to the next class before the bell rings and you're late again—why not take your own time when you can? That's what I did, as soon as I could get away from school.

Our school is called Parkland Middle School, and it's on the corner of School and Union streets. You can look up Union and see the downtown stores. But school lets out on School Street, around the corner, where everyone crowds out the big side doors and the buses pull up, and the parents' cars wait behind the buses in a long line.

If you're going downtown after school, or if you need to go through town to get home like I do, most people head up Union. But I usually left the crowds (where nobody was waiting for me anyway) and went up a shady side lane called Chamber Street. I'd tell myself I liked going my own way. I mean, everybody else in seventh grade had to go everywhere with their friends—they'd walk in their little cliques through the halls, they'd eat together in the cafeteria, and they'd head home (or wherever they went) together after school.

But why attach yourself to the same people every day, with everybody gabbling like a bunch of baby ducks? I didn't mind going by myself, really. Not that much.

Chamber Street leads to the police department. It's a faded brick building, and behind it is the old town parking lot, and across that is the back of Convenience Farms.

Convenience Farms isn't a farm, of course—it's a squat white store with a red plastic roof. It's easily the ugliest building in our downtown, and it has all kinds of good junky food inside. I coasted my bike in from the parking lot and leaned it against the side of the building, and went in to get my root beer.

That's what I always got after school back then, a root beer. My mom gave me $1.10 each morning so I could get one. "There's for your treat," she'd say. (I don't have a dad. He died when I was too young to know. I wouldn't mind having a dad, but I don't.)

I always got a twenty-ounce A&W, in the plastic bottle with the white cap. (I've tried them all. It's the root beeriest!) When I came out of the store with my bottle this eighth grader, Richie Tucker, was leaning against the side of the building, and my bike was lying sprawled on the pavement.

Richie Tucker. *Whoa.* Now he was someone you stayed away from. If you were going somewhere and Richie Tucker was hanging around and he tried to catch your eye, you just didn't look at him. Even I knew that.

But here—I suddenly realized—here was one person who didn't have to be in a group with anybody. Probably nobody was cool enough, or strange or scary enough, to hang around with Richie Tucker anyway.

So I looked at him. He had on this black army jacket, with his hands shoved in the big side pockets. I was thinking maybe I could get a jacket like that, I was wondering where you could buy one, when Richie turned his head and looked at me.

"Is that thing yours?" he asked softly, motioning his head toward the sprawled bike.

"Well, yeah."

"It was in my way."

"Huh?"

"That piece of crap you left there." Richie said this softly and earnestly, nodding at me like we were two very concerned citizens. "It was in *my* way." He put his hands on his hips. "What are you going to do about it? Hmm?"

So I bent over, picked up my bike, and—okay, this was a mistake—shook my finger at it.

"Bad bike," I said. "Bad bike! Don't ever do that *again*!"

See what I mean? Was that *stupid*?

Richie jerked forward like he was coming at me; I hopped on the bike and started pedaling. I nearly dropped the root beer as I rode, a little too fast, up Union Street to get home.

But then for the next couple of days I kept thinking about that black jacket. I wanted to get one. I looked in the Yellow Pages and found an army-navy store, about half an hour away. I could ask my mom to take me, maybe on Saturday. I could tell her I needed it.

Meanwhile, I guess Richie was watching how I went home.

Two days after the incident at Convenience Farms, I was walking home after school. Just this side of the police station there's a narrow, bumpy little driveway. It connects to the parking lot behind the police building, but it isn't the main way into the lot, and hardly anyone uses it. It's shadowed by a line of trees on one side and a windowless brick wall of the police building on the other. I was halfway up the driveway when Richie stepped out from the trees.

He moved to block my way, and smiled. A prickling crackled in the back of my neck. I saw his fist pull back and I wanted to say *No, please! I didn't mean to*, but I just watched his fist drive into my stomach.

I couldn't breathe! I made this panicky *hreek! hreek!* sound, trying to get air. I crumpled up and my heart was pounding and I was shaking all over. Richie grabbed my chin and yanked my face up.

"Nobody mocks me," he said. "You understand? Nobody!"

I went, "*Hreek.*"

Richie stood up and crossed his arms.

"I guess you are nobody," he said. "I guess that's you, huh?"

One tear tipped and fell down my face. Richie's eyes lit up, and he leaned in really close.

"Aw—you got to *cry*, little boy? Are you a little crying nobody?" I turned my face away. He grabbed it and yanked it back.

"Let me tell you how it is, little *boy*. This is not over, okay? This is never over. Every time you turn around—every time you think the coast is clear—you better be watching for me. Okay, little boy? Because you're mine now. You are *mine*. And every time you think you're not . . ."

He jerked his fist back; I grabbed my stomach. Just like that.

He stood up. "Yeah," he said, and smiled. "Just like that."

And then he was gone.

THE MAN WITHOUT FEAR

My mom came home. She was calling hello. I was sitting at my computer, but it wasn't on. The lights were off. I was just sitting there.

"Hi," my mom said from the door to my room.

"Hi."

She walked in. I turned away.

"What's wrong?"

"Nothing."

She reached out and took my chin. She was gentle but it made my face burn, her doing that.

"Russell," she said. "What is it?"

I shook my head free. She leaned back and studied me.

"You look flushed." She felt my cheek with the back of her hand. "Do you feel okay?"

"I'm fine."

"Did something happen?"

"No."

Her palm was on my forehead. "You *are* warm," she said. "I'll just take your temp."

She went away and I was thinking, What's *wrong* with

me? Why do the things I say make people despise me? Why do I say one thing to this one guy, really just trying to be funny, and it makes him that mad?

I didn't get it.

I didn't get anything anymore.

My mom came back and stuck the thermometer in my mouth. I just sat there till she came back again, pulled it out, and peered at it.

"It's normal," she said, shaking it. "Why don't you lie down for a little while? I'll call you when dinner's ready."

I shrugged, but when my mom was gone I went over to my bed and just lay there. I looked up at the ceiling, at nothing. The room slowly got dark.

Middle school, at least our middle school, was basically a place you tried to survive. Last year in sixth grade, when it started, I still had a lot of friends from elementary school— but it was like we had all gone from a family sort of place to this big dim noisy train station. Everybody was rushing around and you hardly knew anybody, and there were predators. They were all over, the predators. Even some of the kids you knew started turning into them. Plus, a lot of kids at our school were changing and making these tight little cliques, and if you didn't fit in somewhere you could be in trouble. One by one, my friends went *pfft*.

And now I knew I was in trouble.

This kind of thing didn't really happen in elementary school. We all grew up together there, we understood each other there. Maybe sometimes a kid would shove you on the playground, or make fun of you for falling down in dodge-ball in gym—or maybe somebody would organize his friends to ignore you for a while . . . but you knew those kids. You knew it wasn't a big deal, because it wasn't.

Middle school is different. Ours is named Parkland

School, as I've said, but most people *in* the school call it Darkland. It's a dark brick pile of an old school, and inside it's murky and crowded until it spreads into a newer wing out back, with flat light from windows up too high to see out of—and the whole place is an obstacle course of kids alert for someone they can pound on or ridicule. If you have no hope of being accepted in a cool clique, or any clique for that matter, you're safest if you can manage not to get noticed at all. And suddenly not getting noticed was all I wanted, starting the day I got singled out by Richie to be the new target of his personal psychological terror campaign.

When I woke in the morning I didn't want to get up. I saw Richie's face like it was right there. By the time I walked into school, my stomach was caving in. I couldn't stop thinking about what he'd said, how every time I turned around he might be there.

I didn't want to turn around. I didn't want to be alone and I didn't want to be in crowds either, but I figured being in crowds was better. Safer. I went to my locker and got out every book I would need all day, and stuffed them in my backpack so I wouldn't have to be out at my locker again.

My backpack felt like a sack of bricks. By third block my shoulder was killing me. I switched sides, then both shoulders were killing me.

Suddenly classrooms were warm protected places, where nothing bad could happen to you. Nothing *really* bad. I watched the clock, hoping I could make time go so slowly it might actually stop. But then the class would be over, and I'd have to go out there again.

Between classes, the Darkland hallways are jammed with people pushing, stepping on your feet 'cause they're jumping up to catch their friend's eye, or just shoving past you in a big elbowing hurry. Most kids just troop along in the herd. That's where I tried to stay.

And all day I didn't see him. But as the afternoon wore on, I started getting into this damp panic about having to make it home after school. I was going to have to go out there. How could I get home?

Then it hit me—I didn't have to go the same way! I could go up Union Street, where everyone could see. He wouldn't try anything where everyone could see, right? I could even go up Bishop Street, which was beyond Union on the far side. I started wondering if I could go all the way on Bishop without being seen from Convenience Farms. I was trying hard to visualize it, to see all the spots of possible exposure.

At the end of school, I came out fast and turned to walk across Union at the corner. Then something made me look back.

Richie was leaning against a tree, just watching me. He didn't move at all; he looked in my eyes, and raised his eyebrows. It was like he knew all along where I was going, even what I was thinking. It felt like he knew everything.

Every day after that was about nothing but whether I would run into Richie, and when, and how he would act. Sometimes he would ignore me, he'd look right past me like I wasn't there. Sometimes he'd look right at me, just watching me—and when I looked back he'd lift his eyebrows that same way. One time he winked, like he and I had a secret. (Which I guess we did, since I sure wasn't telling anyone.)

Another time I passed him in a corridor. I was in a crowd going one way and he was coming down the hall, not in a crowd. Richie was never in a crowd. When I spotted him he was glaring at me—then he sidestepped to block my way. An electric surge bolted through me. Richie's dark eyes were burning; he looked really mad. People flowed past paying no attention.

My chin started to twitch. Then Richie made a scrunched-up, sad face, as if to say: "Oh, are you *scared*?" I stepped around him and just kept walking. My face was burning hot. All the way down the hall I could feel him looking at me. I knew he was laughing at me, in a way that only I could hear.

I started getting stomachaches every morning and bad headaches at two o'clock every afternoon. I didn't tell anybody. Each day I tried to go home a different way, but there were only a few ways you could go. I didn't spend my $1.10 on root beer anymore because I couldn't go near the store. I started buying superhero comics in the drugstore, instead. They made me feel a little better. I would imagine having my own special powers.

My favorite was Daredevil. Even though he's blind, he's The Man without Fear. Courage is his power, and extrasensitive perception. One night in my room I cut out a full-page picture of Daredevil in action, swinging from a rope between two skyscrapers on a dark night way up above the city. I folded the picture in a tight little square and kept it in my pocket all the next day at school, so I could touch it if I needed to. All day, I didn't see Richie even once. I was so happy, by the end of the day, I felt like I was skating.

The next day I had Daredevil in my pocket again. At lunchtime I had to stop at my locker. I couldn't carry all my books around anymore—my shoulders were just too tired. I was late and the long hallway where my locker is, on the way to the lunchroom, was empty. I was starting to turn my combination when, at the end of the corridor, Richie appeared.

He leaned against a locker, looking at me. My fingers

turned slippery. The combination was wrong. I couldn't get the lock open—I couldn't *do* it!

He started walking toward me.

There was total silence except for his footsteps. The hallway was echoing. I wasn't breathing. My fingers were paralyzed.

Beside me, he stopped.

I didn't want to look up. But it was like I had to . . . like he had control.

Richie smiled.

"How you feeling today, little boy?"

My mouth opened, but there was no sound.

"Hey, don't *worry* about it," he said. "You needed to learn something. And you learned. Right?"

"Uh . . ." I blushed.

He leaned closer. "Little boy. Am I *right*?"

Finally I whispered, "Okay."

"What?"

"Yeah."

"*What?*"

"*Yes.*"

"Yeah." He smiled, stepping back. "That's that," he said. He looked me up and down.

"Listen," he said. "You need to stop by the Farms after school today."

"I do?"

"Yeah. You do."

"Why?"

His forehead wrinkled. "Because I *told* you to," he said, patiently.

"Oh."

He started to walk away. "Be there," he said without turning around.

———

That afternoon, I started filling up again with happiness. Hey . . . Richie *smiled* at me! He said that was that!

Maybe he wants to be friends. Maybe I passed some kind of test or something. Maybe that's why he told me to come to the Farms.

Yeah!

I even started thinking about that black army jacket again. I guessed maybe I had earned it now. It'd be like special identification—only he and I would have them. Only we would know.

After school I went up quiet old Chamber again. I walked by the police building and crossed the parking lot. Just when I was coming up to the back of Convenience Farms, the side door opened and Richie stepped out. It was like he knew when I'd be there, like he had extrasensitive perception.

He leaned against the building and flicked his head toward the door.

"Go ahead," he said. "Get your soda."

"Oh. Well, okay. You want one?"

But I didn't have money for two. Why did I . . .

"No," he said, smiling in a funny way. "I don't want one."

I went in and got my root beer. This felt great! I was going to have a soda! Everything was going to be okay. *Really* okay.

When I came back out Richie was still leaning against the wall. He flicked his head again in a motion that told me: *Come over here.*

I went over.

He stuck out his hand. His thumb and fingers were curved, the way you'd hold a bottle. He looked at me. He lifted his eyebrows.

I put the bottle in his hand.

He studied it, frowned, and handed it back.

"It's not *open*," he said.

I turned the white cap. The plastic catches broke, one af-

14

ter another, slowly, like each little *snap* was the only sound in the world.

I gave him the bottle.

He took it and stood up straight, and with his free hand he gripped the front of my shirt. He lifted the bottle over my head, slowly tipped it, and started to pour.

Here's how an ice-cold twenty-ounce A&W root beer feels being poured over your head:

It's cold and wet and it fizzes horribly on your scalp. Down your hair! It fizzes so hard your face hurts—it's like burning, dribbling down the back of your neck, soaking cold the front of your shirt. (Aw no, not *more* . . .) It actually *hurts* on top of your head. You can taste root beer on your tongue, and the drops look golden brown at the tips of your eyelashes. Everything drips. You're already getting sticky.

I just stood there. Richie put the empty bottle in my hand and walked away.

"Recycle," he said, without looking back. "Save the planet."

By the time I got home—in town, people kept turning to look at me—my fingers were sticking together. My shirt was heavy and stuck to my chest, and my hair felt *really* weird. It was plastered down. My underwear was chafing and sticking at the same time.

Then I was inside peeling off the clothes, thankful for once that my mom wasn't home yet. I felt for stuff in the jeans pocket, and pulled out a soaked-brown folded-up square. The Daredevil picture.

I went into the kitchen where the garbage is, and slowly I tore it—the paper fibers just pulled apart—into little wet wads. Then I dropped the wads in the trash.

STREAMING

Well, that was it. That was enough. I had to do something.

I just had no idea what. I mean, what do you do in a situation like this?

It was pointless to ask my mom—it would only make things worse. I do my own laundry after school, so I was able to wash out the evidence.

I had to get myself home from school every day, right? I couldn't send for a helicopter. I couldn't climb into a limo with tinted windows that no one could see in. I liked thinking about that for a while, the limo, but it was also pointless. And I could not avoid or elude Richie just by going different ways.

All of a sudden he had this power over me. He was kind of lording it over me, too—and that, frankly, was what got to me. I didn't want to be friends with this guy, or co-weirdos or whatever. Never mind wearing a stupid jacket; I wanted to figure out how to make him stop.

But how?

The basic trouble was, I had no idea what Richie would do next. I didn't understand him at all, even though most of the time he was all I could think about: where he might be, what mood he would be in . . . what he might do to me. It was kind of an obsession. And that, I suddenly realized, was exactly how he wanted it.

Hey, yeah!

But *why*?

I had no idea. But I wanted to figure it out—I really wanted to. It suddenly occurred to me that I needed advice. Expert advice. I needed to talk to someone who had been in this kind of situation, and every situation like it, many many times before.

I needed to talk . . . with Elliot Gekewicz.

I sat up straight. Yeah!

You know how there's always one kid in school who's the dirty one, one kid who's the smelly one, one kid who throws the ball over the backstop . . . and one kid who it's okay for anybody, absolutely anybody, to trash?

In our school, that last kid was Elliot. Not that he was dirty or smelly—I don't mean that. I wasn't really sure why he was the one, but the fact was that in Parkland School seventh grade, no matter who you were, Elliot Gekewicz was lower on the social scale than you.

He was small, and that wasn't good; he had a horrible name; and he was smart, which only made things worse. And anyway somebody has to be on the bottom, and in our class it was him.

I had known Elliot since we were in kindergarten, and I had seen a lot of stuff happen to him. I never really joined in, but I never tried to stop it either, not that I could have. Kids had done all the usual things: called him names, stomped on his feet, played keepaway with his stuff, hung him by the back of his underpants on the cleat for the climbing rope in gym . . . Kids poured water inside Elliot's backpack—while he was wearing it. They stuffed him in his locker—upside down. They took his milk in the cafeteria, soaked his sandwich with it, squirted in a packet of ketchup, squashed the red-white mess between two trays, took his cookie and walked away eating it while everyone else laughed. Kids would say stuff in the hall when Elliot walked by, like: "Where'd you get that shirt—from a Dumpster? Who cuts your hair—your *mom*?"

Elliot didn't get mad, he didn't cry, and he didn't seem (to me) to ask for it. He wasn't your classic bully magnet. I guess this stuff happened to him because it always had—and because it had to happen to somebody, especially in seventh grade. And he is kind of funny looking. He looks like a little bird with a big bobbing head, scooting across the playground before he's spotted. People called him Bird Boy, sometimes. When he went by in the hall, certain guys would make "cheep cheep" noises.

They did other stuff, too, especially once our class started really getting into the Darkland spirit. Sometimes they played Surround and Pound. They'd trap Elliot on the playground (yes, we still had recess and we were still sent to the playground, in seventh grade), and they'd start closing the circle and shoving him back and forth. He'd try to shoot out between kids, and if they could grab him they'd throw him back. When they closed the circle all the way, they'd shove him like a rag doll between them. Once at recess when Elliot was on the monkey bar by himself, these two guys, Burke Brown and Jon Blanchette, snuck up below and pantsed him. They were the ones who hung him on the cleat, too, actually.

Elliot himself was obsessed with dinosaurs. Had been for years. He was always lugging around big dinosaur encyclopedias, and he had dinosaur stickers on his notebooks—even then, in seventh grade; and when he had any kind of school project he'd relate it to dinosaurs if he could. (You can even do this in math, if you're Elliot. Once when we had to do something on probability, he did "Estimating the Life Span of Triceratops." He said that was probably the last dinosaur to die out, so they know more about it.)

For all I knew, dinosaurs were the only thing Elliot ever thought about. And I could understand this. I mean, if you're Elliot Gekewicz, spending your days lost in your mind among giant prehistoric reptiles probably has a lot more appeal than being awake to the realities of Darkland Middle School.

So anyway, I called him. I had to take a deep breath first, because this was really depressing, in a way. But I told myself I wasn't going to be *friends* with Elliot, I only wanted to ask him a few things. It was like being a detective. I had a mystery, and I was looking for clues.

One of his sisters answered the phone. When I asked for Elliot, there was a long silence. I heard whispering.

Finally she said, "Who is this, please?"

"It's Russell Trainor."

"Oh. O . . . *kay* . . ."

I heard more whispering. The phone was set down . . . then it was picked up and Elliot said, "Hello?"

"Hi," I said. "It's Russell."

"Oh. Hello."

"I had to like pass a security check to get to you."

"Oh. Well . . . I guess I've been getting some not very nice calls."

"Huh. Ah, listen, Elliot. Could I ask you about something? I'm kind of looking for an expert."

"An expert?"

"Well, yeah."

"Me?"

"Oh, definitely."

"Hey, sure!" he said. "When'd you get interested in dinos?"

"It's not *dinosaurs*, Elliot. It is kind of about predators, though. I'm suddenly sort of the target of one. If you know what I mean."

"A predator?"

"Yes."

"Oh."

There was a long pause. Finally Elliot said, "Could we do this Streaming?"

"Uh, well, okay. I guess so. Why?"

"It's more secure."

"Okay, I'll get on-line. What's your address?"

"Troo."

"What?"

"T-R-O-O. For troodon," he said. "It's small but sharp-eyed, with an unusually big brain area. And slashing claws."

"Oh. O . . . kay."

I hung up the phone and turned on the computer.

Our school has a LAN, a local area computer network. Officially it's called SchoolStream, but everyone—every kid, at least—calls it KidNet. Everyone in school has an account, and a password that you keep to yourself. You can access your account from any computer in the school, or from your computer at home, if you have one. You can send any other kid e-mail, and you can send mail to your teachers—you can ask about homework, or other questions. If you're sick they e-mail your homework to you. (Isn't that great?) You can also access encyclopedias, and you can download practice problems for math tests, challenge quizzes for social studies, stuff like that. There's a lot you can do.

One thing is MidStream. We called it Streaming. That's where you and other kids get on together and talk by typing. Other networks call it Chat, or Instant Message, or whatever. Nobody can break into or eavesdrop on your conversation without everyone else knowing about it. I guess that's why Elliot wanted to talk this way: he could tell if anyone else was lurking and listening, like if I was the front person for some new plot to humiliate him.

For your address on our system you get up to five letters. Mine was RussT, which I thought was pretty good.

<RUSST> Are you there?
<TROO> Yes. What predator?
<RUSST> A guy. Eighth grade.
<TROO> Oh.
<RUSST> So when someone's after you, what do you do?

For a minute there was nothing. Then finally:

<TROO> I don't know.
<RUSST> You don't KNOW?
<TROO> Best thing is not to be there.
<RUSST> What if he's always watching? If he always knows where you go?
<TROO> Who IS this?

I sighed. Finally I typed:

<RUSST> R Tucker.
<TROO> Whoa. Tyrannosaur!
<RUSST> Yes. Why's he do it?
<TROO> Don't know. Ask him?
<RUSST> Oh right. How can I get him to stop?
<TROO> You can't.
<RUSST> I CAN'T?
<TROO> Tyranno doesn't stop. Maybe you can get him to find somebody else, but tyrannos don't STOP.

\<RUSST\> Must be SOMEthing I can do.

\<TROO\> Don't be where tyranno is.

\<RUSST\> But he's everywhere. Outsmart him? Somehow?

\<TROO\> Tyrannos are smarter than people think. Proportionately larger brain cavity than any known tyranno prey.

\<RUSST\> What?

\<TROO\> True.

Like I said, Elliot pretty much lived in the reptile ages. I realized if I was going to get anything out of him, I had to go there, too.

\<RUSST\> What DID tyranno prey do?

\<TROO\> Depended on what they could do.

\<RUSST\> Did tyranno prey survive?

\<TROO\> Not many, but hey. Did tyranno survive?

\<RUSST\> But how DID some prey survive? I want to know.

\<TROO\> Meet me in school library tomorrow. After school.

\<RUSST\> Why?

\<TROO\> I can show some stuff.

\<RUSST\> What about tyranno?

\<TROO\> Tyranno never goes in library!

I thought for a minute.

\<RUSST\> OK. After school.

At least I'd be safe, for a little while. And maybe, just maybe, there might be something I could figure out.

POP QUIZ

When I came into the library, Elliot already had a table spread with dinosaur books. I wondered if anyone else ever got to look at the dinosaur books. But who else would want to, in middle school?

He had each book open to a picture. When he looked up, his eyes were bright; then he quickly checked to see if I'd come alone. I thought how Elliot really does look like a bird—especially those tiny birds you see on beaches, darting back and forth on stick legs inches from waves that you think are going to drown them, but never do.

"Look at this," he said before I was even sitting down. He was pointing to a picture of a scrawny dino. It looked like an underfed naked chicken.

"That's gallimimus," he said. "He didn't have teeth or claws, but he could run at forty miles an hour."

"Wish I could," I said, slumping in the chair.

"Now *these* guys, the really big sauropods—the brachiosaurs and the diplocids—they could swing their tails at attackers."

"Elliot . . ."

"I mean probably."

"Huh?"

"We don't know for sure," Elliot said. "It's even possible they could rear up on their hind legs. See this picture? I mean, can you imagine an eighty-ton brachiosaurus pounding down on you? Even a tyranno would have taken off."

"Speaking of tyrannos . . ."

"But I think it's also possible they stayed mostly in the water. They could be in pretty deep water, when you think about it. It's conceivable the big meat-eaters didn't like water. They might even have been afraid of it."

He nodded proudly. "That's one of my own hypotheses. What do you think?"

"Well, I mean, for me . . . swinging tails, deep water, massive tonnage . . ." I shook my head.

"I know—they don't seem like *defenses*," said Elliot. "But the plant eaters used what they had. You know?"

I shrugged. Elliot was opening more books, going right to certain pages. I was starting to wonder what I was doing there.

"Of course, stegosaurs had a spiked tail," he said. "Wouldn't that be something? And ankylosaurs, the armored dinos, they had a round bony club on their tails. Swing it around and, ooh . . . fractured *skull*."

He grinned. I reached over and shut his book. His smile did a puzzled fade.

"I want to know what I can do," I said. Elliot blinked. "You know—in real life? Like I told you?"

He blinked again. I looked around, and leaned over the table.

"Okay," I whispered. "This one guy is bent on basically destroying my life. He wants me to be scared *all* the time.

What do you . . . I mean, no offense, but what do you do in a situation like this?"

Elliot didn't say anything. He just looked down.

"Okay," I finally said. "So . . . you're talking about survival strategies?"

"Yeah! See, like dromaeosaurs. They had a huge sharp claw, just one claw, sticking forward from their back feet. They could slash a bigger dino's belly right open."

"Right open."

"Yes," he said, with a kind of dreamy look.

I sat back while Elliot started rummaging again in his books. At least I'm safe in here, I told myself. Nothing bad can happen in a library.

"Here—see this?"

Elliot held up a picture of a huge striped head. It had a fan growing behind it, and a crown of spikes and a giant nose horn. It was, I had to admit, amazing.

"That's styracosaurus," he said. "He'd just have to turn and *look* at you with that head. I think you'd go find someone else to pick on."

"Yeah, but what about the dinos that had no horns, or armor, or spikes or clubs or claws? And no speed and no hugeness. There were dinos without any of those things, right?"

"Oh, sure. Lots. Big ones *and* little ones."

"So what'd they do?"

"Traveled in herds, mostly. They'd keep the young, small, and weak ones in the middle."

"And that kept the killers away? Really?" I had this sudden mental picture of a whole bunch of kids—skinny kids, little kids, gawky kids, fat kids, kids with funny hair, kids with thick glasses, kids who trip over cracks in the sidewalk. They were trooping through the halls together, all wearing white T-shirts that said: NERD HERD.

I was not in this group. I was definitely not in this group.

"Predators might wait until they could pick off a straggler," Elliot said. "But they probably wouldn't attack a whole crowd."

"Why not?"

"Most predators' brains weren't very large. If a crowd scattered in all directions they probably got disoriented."

I sat back and imagined this big dumb kid charging into the white-shirted crowd—and kids stumbling all over each other, scrabbling on the floor for fallen-off glasses and tossing lunches and electronic equipment out of their backpacks to appease the rampaging beast, who becomes confused and stands there with his big head twitching all around, surrounded by wire-rim glasses and graphing calculators and bologna-and-peanut-butter sandwiches.

"Of course, *tyranno* was different," Elliot said. "He'd lie in some undergrowth near a clearing or a stream bed. When prey came along, he'd charge out with his jaws wide open. Tyranno didn't care how big a herd was! He'd always get somebody."

Suddenly in my mind I saw only Richie's face. He was looking right at me. He raised his eyebrows.

I sagged in my chair.

"Right," I said.

A girl came in and sat down at a table between us and the door. She was in our grade, a girl named Catalina. She was new this year, and different looking: tall and skinny, with big squarish glasses and straight, extremely dark hair, almost black, that hung below her ears. Her face was the color of coffee ice cream, and behind her glasses it was expressionless.

I first noticed that about Catalina, the blank look she had, at the beginning of the year, when she was the new girl being introduced in our social studies class. Ms. Hogeboom, who knew a Learning Opportunity when she saw one, asked the new girl to tell a little about herself.

The new girl stood up. People started whispering.

"I am from near Manila. In the Philippines," she said, and sat down. The whispers turned into giggling.

"There's no need to stand when you're called, Catalina," Ms. Hogeboom said. "Is that what students do in the Philippines?"

Catalina started to stand again, but stopped partway. "In my school, yes," she said, bent over like a grasshopper. More giggles erupted. She sat down fast.

"*Excuse* me, please," Ms. Hogeboom said loudly. When the class settled down she said, "Now, Catalina. How did you happen to come to this country? You don't have to stand."

"My father is from Ohio," she said. "He was in Manila for his company. He decided to come back."

"Oh. I see," Ms. Hogeboom said, and she turned to the rest of the class with a pleased expression, as if to say: See how totally we can embarrass someone when we all work together? Because by then half the kids in class—mostly the girls—were whispering and giggling again. Everyone was looking at Catalina, who sat bolt upright and looked straight ahead, with no expression at all.

Catalina sat down now at the library table and unloaded a bunch of books from her shoulder bag. I was watching her over Elliot's shoulder. He was deep in his books. Catalina opened a book and then she was deep in hers, too. Through the doorway behind her came a gaggle of seventh-grade girls.

There were four of them, walking close together and almost tiptoeing like they were holding their breaths. They came our way stealing quick glances at Catalina, who sat with her back to them. In the center of the group was Bethany DeMere.

Bethany DeMere is the ruler of the top clique of seventh-grade girls. She's popular, and she's one of those people who knows just what to say to cut you down. A lot of times she doesn't say anything—she just looks away and shakes her head so her hair ripples down her back. She has this long, wavy blond hair that she knows is pretty eye-catching. If she wants to show you that you are not worth seeing or hearing, she shakes her hair as she turns away and sighs or rolls her eyes at somebody who *is* worth seeing and hearing. Of course, to her I did not exist. I didn't even have hair-shaking status.

Bethany and her crew crowded past us looking pressurized, like they could barely contain themselves about whatever they were up to. They went into the stacks and I heard whispering, and stifled giggling.

Before long Catalina stood up and walked over to the catalog computers. About two seconds after she was gone, the DeMere clique came out from the stacks. The girls quick-stepped till they were just passing Catalina's books and notebook, where one of them lifted her arm above the table's edge.

She dropped a folded piece of paper beside Catalina's books. It bounced once, and then lay there.

As soon as the girls had veered out the door they burst into fierce laughter. Then their fast steps faded down the hall.

Elliot was still burrowing in his books. "Hey, look at this," he said.

I held up my hand. His forehead crinkled. I put my finger to my lips, and pointed over his shoulder.

"What?" he whispered. I pointed at the note.

"What?" he said. "That?"

I nodded.

Catalina came back. Elliot shrugged and turned back to his books. I lowered my head, but I still watched.

At her table Catalina stopped. She definitely spotted the paper, and she froze. Then she carefully, steadily gathered up her books, slid them into the shoulder bag, slung it on her shoulder and walked out.

She left the folded paper on the table.

"Psst," I said.

Elliot looked up. I motioned with my head over his shoulder, toward the paper. He twisted his head to look, then turned back and shrugged.

"Grab it," I whispered.

"Why?"

"Because you're closer."

"But why?"

"Just . . . I just want to see it. All right?"

He looked around, ducked to the table, grabbed the paper, and ducked back.

With one finger he slid it over. It was folded neatly, tightly, carefully. I slowly unfolded it.

It said:

Pop Quiz
Q: Is there a special school for people from someplace weird who look like Olive Oyl and are the color of diareea?
A: WE SURE HOPE SO!

On the side one of them wrote *"(in Popeye)"* with an arrow pointing over to *Olive Oyl*, just to make it clear.

Elliot looked up. "Where'd this come from?"

"You know Bethany DeMere."

"Well. Not really."

"Elliot."

"What?"

"This sucks, man."

He squinted at it. "I don't think diarrhea is spelled right," he said. "I'm pretty sure it has two *r*'s."

I stood up. "Come on," I said.

"Huh?"

"Come on—quick!"

"But what about the tyrannosaur?"

"Never mind about the tyrannosaur!"

I was out the door. Elliot came scrambling after me.

ANATOSAURS

I popped into the hall in time to see a set of fire doors closing slowly, down at the end. Through their glass I saw the top of a dark head bobbing down the stairs.

"Come on," I said again.

"Where?" said Elliot. "Why?" His eyes were darting around, alert for danger. But the hall was empty.

"Look. Do you like to see people getting treated . . . like you get treated?"

Elliot looked carefully at me. "No."

"So let's just go talk to her."

"Talk to who?" Elliot tilted his head like a puppy. I realized: He'd been deep in his dinos. He hadn't seen anything.

"You know that new girl, Catalina?"

"The tall skinny girl?"

"Yeah."

"With the big glasses?"

"Yes."

"She came in the library."

"Yes."

"She looks kind of like a salamander," Elliot mused, his eyes unfocusing. "Like a really long newt."

"Okay. Bethany and her pals came in and dropped that note so she would read it."

He blinked. "They did?"

"Yeah."

"Did she?"

"No. But I think she knew what it was. It looked like maybe this was not the first time."

Elliot nodded slowly. "Well . . . so?"

"She went downstairs. At least I think she did. Let's just go talk to her."

"Why?"

Here we were again, back where we started. And actually, I wasn't sure why.

"Okay," I said. "You know how you were talking about those defenseless dinosaurs? There were big ones, little ones . . ."

"Sure—like the duckbills. Anatosaurs. They didn't even have claws. Ever see a picture?"

"Yeah. I mean, no. But what I *mean* is, if one of those defenseless ones was pretty much all by themselves, they'd be in a lot more trouble, right?"

He nodded. "They'd be pretty much dead. Sooner or later."

"Right."

"There are fossils in Montana that show how duckbills grouped together around their nests. They protected their young. Only dinosaurs known to have done that."

Geez. But I kept trying. "So what if this new girl is separated from her regular group, or herd, or whatever? What if we just went and, you know . . . checked up on her?"

"You mean if *we* were like anatosaurs?"

"Well. I don't mean . . ."

"Hey, sure! Let's go!" Elliot said, and he went scooting down the hall.

The basement of Darkland School is dim and dungeony, but it's where the "special" rooms are, so it's not that bad. The art room, the music room, and the computer lab are all down here. Looking for Catalina, we checked around. The art room's paint-spattered tables were full of plastic bottles with yellow and blue and red paint caked around the tops. Nobody was in there. The computer lab was full, as usual, of kids hunched before beeping machines. But there was no spectacled girl with almost black hair.

Next was the boiler room. Its heavy louvered door was shut.

"She could be in there," Elliot said.

"The *boiler* room?"

"Well? She could . . ."

An awful noise—"*Sqwer . . . ONK!*"—came from somewhere.

I said, "What was *that*?"

Elliot perked up. "The crested duckbill might have sounded just like that!" he said. "It had this long curving hollow bone crest that reared up and back from its nasal cavity. Kind of like a horn, you know? It must have sounded . . ."

"*SqueeeeEEEEEEE—HONK!*"

"Like *that*," he whispered, awed.

"The practice room," I said. "Come on."

Down here in the basement, across from the band room, there's this mazelike music practice room, full of cubicles. They ought to be soundproof, the cubicles, but they're just padded panels about five feet high. I've seen the same thing in the bank. The kids practicing can't see each other, but they can *hear* each other. Sometimes when you go by there it sounds like a demented barnyard.

This time the practice room looked empty. We started exploring among the cubicles when, from farther in: *"Sqwa-REEEEEE! Sqwaa . . . HAWWK!"*

We followed the aftershocks till we saw Catalina.

She was sitting hunched over in a blue plastic chair with her back to us, holding a big brass sax. Her head dipped and her shoulders clenched; she got ready to blow again.

"No!" Elliot said. "Wait!" He clapped his hands on his ears and staggered backward.

Catalina turned just as Elliot stumbled into a chair behind him that was on rollers—so it rolled, and tipped and then crashed into a music stand, and both the stand and the chair clattered into a booth while Elliot toppled over, caught another chair with a flailing arm, and that chair—which had music folders piled up on it—flipped and dumped on top of him. The chair's casters were spinning. The folders sifted across the floor. Elliot lay at the bottom of the wreckage.

I grinned and shook my head. Amazing. Catalina's eyes, magnified behind her glasses, were wide.

"Uh . . . hi," Elliot said. He waved.

"Hello."

"You're *terrible*."

Catalina looked sadly at the sax. She nodded. We waited for her to say something, but she didn't.

"I tried to play the trombone once," I offered. "I even took lessons. But I always sounded like a really drunk moose."

Catalina looked at me. "How does a drunk moose sound?"

I shrugged. "Got a trombone?"

She smiled, almost without moving the rest of her face.

"Russell," Elliot said. "Would you please get this thing off me?"

"Okay." I set the chair on its wheels. Elliot struggled up till he was sitting. Catalina looked at her sax.

"I'm only renting it for a month, to try it," she said. "I probably sound like a really weird donkey."

"Elliot says it's more like a . . . what was it?"

"A crested duckbill."

Catalina said, "Anatosaur."

Elliot's face lit up. "Yeah! And those crests were *honkable*. They'd blast the forest when a predator was coming."

"I think they were cute," Catalina said.

"You . . . you do?"

"Yes." She nodded. "Like edmontosaurus. That soft, dumb-looking face. You'd like to pet him."

Elliot scrambled up amid the debris. "I know! He didn't have the crest," he explained to me, "but he might have had a big skin balloon on top of his head. He could maybe inflate it, to honk or call or something."

"Yes," Catalina said. "Can you imagine all those honks and toots and blasts, all singing through the forest? It must have been incredible. A whole communication system."

I shook my head, smiling in amazement. "A meeting of the minds," I said.

That's when Catalina saw the folded-up paper in my hand.

Her face shrank into a blank mask. She turned away and started yanking apart her saxophone and packing it in the case.

"What?" Elliot said. "What's wrong?"

"If you came here to bring that to me," she said without turning around, "just leave it. Wherever you want."

"Leave what? Bring what?" Elliot looked at me.

I held up my hand with the note.

"Oh," he said. "Hey—we didn't . . ."

The case snapped shut. Catalina snatched it up by the handle and started sidling past us. She was a head taller than me.

"Hey," I said, "we didn't bring this to give it to you. We came looking for you 'cause we think it sucks."

She stopped.

"Yeah," Elliot said. "We're duckbills, too."

"Well," I said, "I mean, you—"

She said, "What?"

"We're kind of like the plant eaters in a swamp of killer reptiles," Elliot said, and he grinned.

"Well," I said. "Not *all*—"

"My favorite was diplodocus," she said. "I think he was extremely cute."

Elliot said, "Cute? He was thirty feet tall!"

Catalina smiled. "That's right."

We were walking up the stairs together.

"Did every plant eater have its predator?" I asked.

"Some had more than one," Catalina said.

"That's me," said Elliot.

"You have more than one predator?"

"I have 'em *all*." Elliot looked at me. "Don't I?"

"Pretty much," I said.

"Russell just has one tyrannosaur."

"I'm Russell," I said. "This is Elliot."

"I'm Catalina."

"We know," Elliot said. "I think Bethany and her friends are like those medium-sized meat-eaters that hunted in packs. You know, velociraptor?"

"From the movie," Catalina said. "With the slashing claw."

"Yeah! And I'm like troodon."

"I don't know him."

"He wasn't very big—but he also had slashing claws."

"Oh, that's you all right," I said. We were walking down the hall toward the main door. Suddenly I thought about what was waiting for me outside.

I stopped. "So I want to know what *we* can do," I said. "For real."

"He means about the predators," Elliot told Catalina. "He thinks there's something we can do."

"Well, why not? There must be something," I said. "Some weakness. Some strategy. I mean, all those helpless dinosaurs weren't really helpless, were they? They all created some strategy for surviving."

"All the dinosaurs died," Catalina said.

"Okay. Right. But . . . what about those furry little characters? The mammals and stuff. The platypuses."

Elliot said, "The *platypuses?*"

"Yeah—the creatures that did survive. They created some strategy, right? For surviving."

"They didn't," Catalina said. "Evolution did."

"Right. Yeah. So let's evolve."

Elliot squinted at me. "You want us to become weird little furry mammals, squatting in mud to lay eggs?"

Catalina smiled. "They are duckbills," she said.

"Hey. Yeah!"

"Aw, just *stop* it," I snapped. They stopped.

"You know what?" I said, backing away. "I'm not really into this, okay? I mean, I've got a real problem—and he's most likely out there right now, waiting for me. And *don't* you say anything about tyrannosaurs.

"It's not a fantasy world, you know? We can't just pretend we're somewhere else in between getting clobbered."

Elliot looked down. I started to feel bad, but still.

"I was just thinking maybe you could help me figure out some stuff," I said to them, more quietly now. "Like why this one person is doing certain things, and what I could do to get him to stop. But I guess . . . I don't know. I guess it wasn't very realistic.

"Anyway," I said to Catalina, "it was nice to meet you." I was thinking she and Elliot could be friends. That would be good for them.

I turned for the big doors, and saw the outside light leaking in between them. I started to get the fear.

"We could study them," Catalina said, behind me. "Like scientists."

I stopped. "Who?"

"The predators," Elliot said. "Yeah."

I turned back slowly. "How?"

Catalina shrugged. "We could experiment."

"Yeah!" said Elliot.

"How?"

"I'm not sure," Catalina said. "Maybe we could do certain things differently ourselves. With them. We could watch what happens."

"I keep trying to walk different ways home, but he always finds me when he wants to," I said. "I just wish I knew why me. Why does he pick me?"

"Why don't you ask him?" she said. She didn't even know who I meant—but it was like she didn't need to. She understood.

"Yeah!" Elliot said. "Like a scientist. Maybe you could figure him out."

"I guess it's possible," I said.

"It's something to do," said Catalina.

"It might get me killed."

"No, no," Elliot said. "We're looking for something *different*."

I grinned and shoved open the outside door. I stood there blinking in the late day's light.

"We'd be like detectives," Elliot said, coming up beside me. "Solving strange mysteries."

The buses were gone by now, and the parents' cars—and the kids. *He* wasn't around. And I was halfway home before I realized that with Elliot and Catalina, I really hadn't said anything too clanky or weird. Not that it would stand out if I did. Not in that group.

EXPERIMENT

That night when we were doing the dishes, I told my mom about Elliot and Catalina.

"The thing is," I said, "they're kind of nerdy."

She leaned against the counter. Crossed her arms. Uh-oh.

"Why do you say that? Aren't they just people?"

"Yeah, yeah."

"Well?"

"Never mind, Mom, okay?"

"No, really. What makes someone nerdy? I never got that."

"That's 'cause you're, you know—a scientist." (My mom's an environmental engineer. She works for the state.)

"Oh, so *I'm* a nerd?" She smiled. "Is that it—if you're scientific?" She rinsed a plate and handed it to me.

"Well . . . not exactly. It's more that people just know they don't fit in." I slotted the plate in the dishwasher rack.

"Well, how important is fitting in?" she said. "I mean, really?"

I just looked at her. Is this where we get cluelessness—from our parents? Is it genetic? Am I doomed?

I shrugged. "I don't know."

"All right, it is important. I do remember. But, I mean, are these nice kids? These two?"

"Well, yeah. I mean, they're kind of out there, but I think they're okay. Then . . . then there's this other kid. He's older, and bigger. He's sort of into scaring me."

Her head jerked around. "What do you mean, scaring you?"

"Well, he's basically a predator. And I'm his latest prey."

She leaned back against the counter. Crossed her arms again.

"Why?"

"That's the thing—I don't really know." I put in the last glasses and shut the dishwasher door. "These other two kids, they think I should just ask him."

She grinned. "You mean, take a scientific approach?"

I looked down. "Yeah. That's nerdy, isn't it?"

"No, actually I don't think it's nerdy at all. If this boy's been bothering you and you march right up and ask him *why*, I think that would be fairly courageous."

"Yeah? You think I should do it?"

"Well, maybe not."

"What?"

"I just don't know," she said. "If this boy's dangerous, maybe you should stay away from him. Can't you just avoid him?"

"I've been trying to avoid him for days. It's not working. I need to figure out how I can get him to stop. What if I tried this, as like an experiment? Asking him why?"

She shrugged. "Well, what's the worst that could happen?"

"I don't know." I really didn't. "I guess he could tell me to shut up and go away."

"Maybe he'd go away," my mom said as she turned off the kitchen lights.

"I'd be fine with that," I said, and my mom and I laughed.

<RUSST> I want to know what to say. How to ask him.
<TROO> You're asking ME?

I shook my head at the screen. Who else would I ask?

<RUSST> Didn't you ever want to ask anybody why? Why you?
<TROO> Yes.
<RUSST> But you never did?
<TROO> No.
<RUSST> What would you ask if you could?
<TROO> How about . . . How would you prefer to die?

Whoa. Maybe Elliot was better off staying in the Jurassic Age. I started typing quickly.

<RUSST> But what would be . . . scientific approach?
<TROO> Have a theory. Test it.
<RUSST> OK, what theory?
<TROO> That he does it cause somebody does it to him?
<RUSST> WHAT? Nobody does it to Richie.
<TROO> Then what?
<RUSST> Well . . . he likes it that I get scared. He likes it BECAUSE I get scared.
<TROO> Gives him power.
<RUSST> Yes. Control. I thought about that.
<TROO> If you ASK him, does that take away control?
<RUSST> What, like magic?
<TROO> No. But he's not dominating you if YOU ask HIM.
<RUSST> Maybe.

<TROO> Will you try it?
<RUSST> Don't know.
<TROO> Try it, OK?
<RUSST> Why?
<TROO> I just hope you try it.

I thought about it.

<RUSST> I'll TRY to try it.
<TROO> OK try.

Next day. After school. I took a deep breath and started up Chamber Street.

He was leaning on the far side of a tree, right by the street. As soon as I saw him a wall went up inside me. I couldn't get past it—I just couldn't. Then he turned and raised his eyebrows, and he smiled that smug smile.

That did it. I walked up to him.

"Why?" I said.

Richie's eyebrows lifted again, but more in surprise. He leaned in close.

"Are you speaking to me?"

I stepped back. "Well, yeah. I just wonder why. Why me? What'd *I* do?"

He leaned in closer. "You know what you did."

"Okay . . . yeah. But you got me back, right? So how come it's not over?"

He got snarly. "I told you—it's never over."

"But *why*?"

He tilted his head. "Are you going to cry again, little boy?"

But I wasn't. "Why does it matter so much to you?" I asked. "Do you need somebody to fixate on, or what?"

He leaned back. "What the hell do you mean, *fixate*?"

"That's what I'm trying to figure out."

He shoved me. "You don't figure out crap, all right? There's nothing to figure out. I do what *I* want to do. All right?"

"But why?"

He snorted. "Kid, whenever you think you're smart, you're stupid. Okay? Whenever you think you're smart. Think about that."

"I don't think I'm smart."

"Well, neither do I." He poked me in the chest. "I think you're *nobody*. 'Cause you are nobody."

He leaned in close and started talking slow. "And if you ever—and I mean *ever*—talk back to me again . . ."

"What if somebody did this to you?" I said. "How would you feel if somebody wanted to make your life hell and you didn't know why? How would you . . ."

WHAM!

A bone-bashing fist hit my face. The sky swam . . . my head clonked on the street.

I curled up, arms around my head. My face pounded. My nose was pouring something wet and dark on the pavement.

I looked up . . . Richie was hazy, standing there wavering. Everything went shimmery, whitish. I felt sick.

Someone picked me up by my armpit and one leg and carried me off the street. Laid me down. The grass was cool and soft. The person's feet went away, then came back, and my backpack was dumped beside me.

The feet hurried off. I looked up. It was Richie, quickly walking away.

Somehow I staggered home, holding to my face some blood-soaked napkins left over in my backpack from the lunches my mom made. In the bathroom I sat on the floor a long time. I just sat there. My face was pulsing; every pulse hurt.

Finally I got up. I peered at myself in the bathroom mirror. There was a multicolored area around my left cheek-bone, below my eye—mostly shades of purple, gray, and blue, with some red crinkles. I wet a washcloth and very carefully wiped off the rest of the blood. Then everything went whitish and hazy again. I stumbled into my room and fell on the bed.

I felt a nudge. A hand on my shoulder was gently rolling me up.

"Russell? What are you . . . oh my god."

She sat down. I inched up on the pillow.

"He hit you. That boy *hit* you."

I nodded. That hurt. She bent to look.

"How is it?" I said.

"Well . . . interesting colors."

"That's what I thought."

"What *happened*?"

"I asked him some questions."

"He didn't like that."

"No. I mean, at first he was just being a jerk, but then . . ." I touched my face. "Ow." The low, thick throbbing was coming back.

My mom stood up. "What's his name?" she said.

"Richie Tucker. Why?"

She stood there thinking, like she hadn't heard me. "That boy's got a lot more problems than you do," she finally said. "And one of them's about to be me." She walked to the door.

"Mom."

"Yes?"

"Don't."

"Don't what?"

"Don't call. Don't do anything."

"Don't do *anything*? Why not?"

" 'Cause it'll just make a mess. I mean, think about it.

45

Everybody's going to know about this . . ." I pointed to my face. "And if my mom comes in yelling or does whatever . . ."

"I'm not going to yell or do whatever."

"So just don't, okay? I'm all right. Really."

She looked at me, tilting her head. Her eyes got wet.

"Baby, I'm sorry." She started crying. "I'm sorry. I feel so responsible."

"Why?" I said. "You didn't do anything."

"I said, *What's the worst that could happen?*" She shook her head. "I should have known."

"How?"

She blew her nose, and shrugged.

"Because he's a guy," she said.

"I think he felt bad."

"You do? Why?"

"He helped me. After he hit me."

"He helped you?"

I nodded. "He carried me off the street."

She just looked at me, her mouth open. Her face got red. "He hit you and you were lying on the *street*?"

"Well . . . yeah."

She stood up. "I'm sorry," she said. "I'm not doing nothing. If one adult did this to another, he'd be in jail. Why should it be different for kids?"

"I don't know. 'Cause we're kids?"

"A kid like that is going to keep on doing the same things to people, even when he's grown up. Unless someone calls him on it."

She went out. She came back with an ice bag.

"Hold this here, nice and gently," she said. "I'm going to go call the principal."

"*Don't.*"

"I'm going to call her at home, okay? Very quietly. I just think she should know."

46

She went out. I lay there for a while with the ice bag. After a while I went over and turned on the computer. A message from Elliot popped up right away. I told him what happened, and what my mom said.

<RUSST> She's telling the principal.
<TROO> Don't worry. Principal won't do anything.
<RUSST> How do you know?
<TROO> She never does. She's weird. How's your face?
<RUSST> Not broken.
<TROO> Can you type OK?
<RUSST> With my face?
<TROO> No I mean can you type?

I stared at the screen. Okay, well, Elliot's in an alternate universe.

<RUSST> I guess. Why?
<TROO> Type what happened? Send it to me?
<RUSST> What for?
<TROO> It was an experiment—you need to notate the results. That's what scientists do.
<RUSST> So now we're scientists?
<TROO> We're not punching bags. Will you write it? Just write what happened.
<RUSST> OK. I guess.
<TROO> Stream it to me. Attach the file to a message. Simple. Do it?
<RUSST> OK OK!

I didn't really feel like it, and I had homework to do. But I logged off, looked at the screen, and started to type.

THE WEIRD GIRL

"It felt kind of good, writing that," I said the next day.

"Well, it was good," Elliot said. "I read it."

"What was good?" said Catalina.

We were at the lunchroom table in the corner by the sandwich counter, Bun Appetit. The usual lunchtime racket was clattering off the walls.

"He wrote down what happened to him," Elliot told her. "He just wrote the facts."

"Did you ever try it?" I asked. "I mean, after somebody did something to you."

Elliot just looked down. He didn't say anything. Finally, I said, "So . . . what are you going to do with it?"

"Keep it! Hold on to it."

I didn't get it. "What for?"

"I don't know—'cause it's information. We're scientific investigators, right? We need to collect data. That's what . . ."

"What scientists do. I know. That's what *you* say."

Catalina was sitting straight backed next to Elliot, staring off like she was only partly there. I thought, What a pair.

"So," Elliot said to her. "Maybe you could do the next experiment."

Catalina blinked. "What?"

"Well, I mean . . . you could say something different to Bethany. Or do something different. See what happens."

Catalina's eyes bulged. She whispered, "I can't."

"Why not?"

"Well . . . I couldn't just go talk to her. She has never spoken to me. She only talks about me."

"She does?"

I said, "Why you?"

Catalina shrugged. "I don't know."

"Well," Elliot said, "what does she say?"

"I told you—she doesn't say it to me."

Elliot turned my way.

"Don't look at me," I said. "I don't understand anything."

Elliot just sat there twirling the straw in his milk carton. Nobody said anything.

"Hey," I said. "What if we listened to her?"

Elliot said, "To who?"

"To Bethany."

"Bethany talks to you?"

"Of course she doesn't—that's just it. What if we listened anyway?"

Elliot peered at me. "How?"

"Look," I said, leaning over the table, "Bethany DeMere does not see or hear us. Right?"

"Yeah."

"She doesn't want to see or hear us. Right?"

He shrugged. "I guess."

"So what if we kind of . . . shadowed her? We could be hanging around, in the hallways and stuff—just close enough to hear what she says." I leaned closer. "We could observe her in her *natural habitat*."

Elliot's eyes twinkled. "Like scientists," he breathed.

"Yes."

"Maybe we'll find her weakness," he said to Catalina. "Maybe we can figure out what really gets to her."

Catalina shrugged. But, staring off, she smiled, too.

Of course my face had been noticed. My eye was black and purple, with red accents. Fairly gruesome. When I came into homeroom that morning there were whispers all over. Heads turned as I ducked into my seat.

"Whoa, Trainor. What happened?" said Big Chris Kuppel, beside me. Our homeroom was a science classroom, so we sat in pairs at black lab tables.

I shrugged.

"Get beat up by your cat?"

"No."

"Stumble into the shower nozzle?"

"No."

"Miss your mouth with the milk bottle?"

"No!"

"Okay, I give up," Chris said. His head looked like an acorn. He had his hair cut in this short bowl shape, which looked a little goofy because he was big. Chris and a kid at the next table, Jon Blanchette, were in the group of three guys who were Elliot's primary tormentors. They used to wait for Elliot after school. He called them the Jock Rots.

"So what did happen?" Chris said. "Or maybe I shouldn't ask."

I shrugged. "I got slugged."

"You? By who?"

"Richie Tucker."

Chris's face bulged. "Richie Tucker slugged *you*?"

"Uh-huh."

"How come?"

I smiled at him. " 'Cause I'm so bad," I said. "I angered him."

Big Chris leaned over and whispered the news to Blanchette, whose expression arced upward in the coolly humorous way he had. Then Blanchette tilted to pass the word across the aisle. In about one minute the whole class was buzzing again. Even the girls were glancing at me. It was kind of neat, in a way, although I couldn't help wondering if the only way I would ever get to be somebody in seventh grade was by getting myself brutalized.

My mom did call the principal, but Elliot was right—nothing happened at all. Meanwhile, I didn't see Richie the whole day. But I wasn't so scared of him, either—which was weird, considering my face. I actually felt that as long as I looked this way, he would probably leave me alone. I wasn't sure why I felt that, but I did.

When school ended we were looking for Bethany, Elliot and me. Down the hall we saw Catalina open her locker. Then she reached down and picked up a piece of paper. It was folded up tight, like the note in the library. Without opening it she let it drop to the floor. She stood there a minute, like she was thinking, but you couldn't tell anything by her face. Then she stooped to pick up the paper again.

As soon as she had it open and started reading it she turned deep red and dropped it. Right then a group of girls swept past us from behind. In the center was Bethany. As they walked toward Catalina, we started following.

The girls were whispering behind their hands. When they were almost to Catalina, they slowed down. Bethany rippled her hair and started talking, a little too loud. "Janice invited *everyone* worth inviting. Her dad rented the Holiday Inn pool. Any seventh-grade girl who didn't get invited is a total *loser*."

They were just passing Catalina, who stood clutching her bookbag, staring hard into her locker. The girls bubbled over in hand-clamped whispering and laughter as they gaggled off down the hall.

We stopped at Catalina's locker.

"What a bunch of . . . I don't even know what," Elliot said to her.

She just stared into the locker.

"You know what? They're like sharks," I said to Catalina's back. "Cold-blooded and always moving."

She didn't say anything.

"You don't want to know them anyway," Elliot said.

Catalina started yanking books out of her locker and jamming them in her bag. She slung the bag on her shoulder, then she bent down and grabbed the paper off the floor.

"You want to know about her?" she said. Her face was very red. "You want to know what kind of . . . stuff she comes up with? Here." She shoved the paper in my hand. "You can have this one, too."

She slammed her locker and started to go. Then she turned back. "In fact, why don't you keep *all* these from now on? You can share them with everybody."

She whirled and stalked away. I stood there with the paper in my hand.

"What'd *we* do?" Elliot said.

I shrugged. I started unfolding the note, with him looking over my shoulder.

It was patterned with tight little folds, to make it small and narrow. Bethany must have had one of her friends slip it through the louvers on the locker door, and then they all waited till Catalina found it so they could walk by and say that lousy party stuff so she'd hear it right then. Which, when you put it all together, was a very nasty little plan.

But then we read the note:

Everybody knows why the weird girl had to leave
where she came from.
Because she was so EASY
the boys wouldn't even look at her in public anymore.
She learned it from her mother. They have no morals
there.
That's why the weird girl doesn't belong here AT ALL.

"Holy crap," Elliot said. "Holy crap."

I folded up the paper and put it in my pocket. Elliot started stalking around the hall.

"What would they do that for?" he was saying. "What would they *say* that for?"

"I don't know. 'Cause they're girls?"

"Holy crap," he kept saying. "Holy crap!"

"All right, Elliot. It's okay."

"It's not okay!" he yelled at me. "All right? It's *not*!"

"Okay. Take it easy."

"I'm *not* gonna take it easy!" He was walking in strange, fast little circles. "I really hate this. How could they *say* that about her?"

I didn't understand this then, but now I think I do. Catalina was (along with me, more or less) the first kid who had been nice to Elliot in a very long time. She liked dinosaurs, and she was his friend. He never got mad about the rotten things kids did to him—I think he kept how he felt about all that stuff down deep, like he'd made a wall inside himself. But when those girls did such a nasty, evil thing to his new friend, the wall crumbled. It all started coming up.

"Listen," I said, "let's go outside. All right? Let's just go outside." I took Elliot's elbow and steered him out the doors.

He kept saying, "I can't believe this. I can't *believe* this!"

We were walking up Union Street. Elliot was walking fast. Suddenly he turned to me and said, "You think she won't ever talk to us again?"

The cars were loud, going by. I said, "What?"

"Maybe she won't talk to us anymore!"

"Why? We didn't do anything."

"I don't know," he said. "Because we know?"

"Know what—that stuff they wrote? Look, they made it up," I said. "Just forget about it."

Elliot stopped in front of an old red church that's a part-time thrift shop. On the front steps it had some swollen cardboard boxes with old clothes spilling out of them. I remember that, 'cause that's where Elliot went nuts.

"I'm not going to forget about it!" he yelled at me. "I'm sick of what people do, okay? *I'm SICK of it!"*

"Okay. Elliot, it's okay."

"Stop saying that! It's *not* okay—*IT SUCKS!* Somebody has to do something!" His face was all strange. *"Somebody has to pay!"*

I just stood there. Elliot turned and started walking fast and jerky through the yard of the old church, heading for his house. Then he turned back and yelled at me one more time.

"Somebody has to!" he hollered, standing on that scraggly lawn. Then he took off.

BIRD BOY

✳I've never figured out if Elliot planned to do what he tried to do the next day to a particular group of people, or if he was just ready to go after the first people who picked on him. Or if he had any plan at all. I've never asked him.

But it was the Jock Rots. It makes sense, in a way. After all, they were his number-one tormentors.

There were three Jock Rots, as I've said. After school they were always together, back then. Burke Brown was short, dark haired, and sharp faced—he was wicked fast and aggressive in sports, and sarcastically mocking with anyone who wasn't. Jon Blanchette was the golden boy. He was golden haired and liquid good at every sport there is, and at pretty much anything else. Blanchette always looked like he was about to laugh, either at how easy life was for him, or at you. Burke needed to be cool—Blanchette just was.

And there was Big Chris. Big Chris was big and acorn headed but not dumb at all, actually, just kind of loyal and there. At least, until this happened, he was there. After what happened that day, Big Chris never acted quite the same.

Anyway. To go home, Elliot walks past the park. It doesn't

have a name, it's just the park. It has tennis and basketball courts beside the road, and behind them a big open field, then a wooden footbridge over the river to the Little League fields. The river is not very big or wide, but it's full of big rocks below the bridge, where a short little waterfall pours down. In summer kids mess around a lot down there below the fall and the rocks, where the water smooths out.

All day Elliot had acted edgy, fidgety, like a nervous little bird. Catalina wouldn't look at him or me or anyone. I knew they were both really upset. I had a bad feeling about almost everything.

So when Elliot left school, I followed. I didn't turn on Chamber, I didn't watch for Richie. I just kept an eye on my friend.

The Rots were on the basketball court at the park. When they spotted Elliot coming they sauntered out in the street.

Casually they surrounded him. Blanchette slapped him hard on the shoulder; Elliot stumbled and Blanchette grinned. Then, from behind, Burke started unzipping his backpack. Elliot reached in his jacket pocket and pulled something out.

He took a step back. The something was dark and not very big, hanging from his hand. The three Rots were just standing there looking when Elliot swung this thing over-hand, and it came down and smacked Burke on the fore-head.

Burke screamed and went down on one knee. He was holding his forehead and face in both hands. Blanchette looked at Burke and he looked at Elliot, then he stepped to-ward Burke. Elliot started to swing the thing at Blanchette, but Blanchette saw it so he jumped forward, grabbed Elliot's hand, and jerked his own head back so the thing whizzed past his face. I just stood there, still a ways away; it was so unbelievable I just kept watching, like this was some weird scene on TV.

Blanchette grabbed the thing and yanked hard. Elliot stumbled but held on; Blanchette pulled *really* hard and Elliot let go and fell in the gravel on the roadside. But he scrambled right up. He stood there, kind of crouched. Burke was howling, down on his knee. He opened his hands and looked for blood or something. Then he looked up at the object in his friend's hand.

From where I was it looked like a little hanging dark thing, with a bulge at the end. Elliot was crouched like he was ready to run when Blanchette dropped the odd little weapon and lunged for him. Elliot tried to take off but Blanchette grabbed him. Big Chris grabbed him, too. They held him, their big kids' hands clamped on each little arm, as Burke slowly got up and stooped over to the dark object on the ground.

He picked it up and looked at it. It was limp. Something spilled out of it, onto the gravel.

Burke flung the thing down and flew into Elliot's face. He was screaming at him, screaming all the curse words you could say—then Elliot started screeching right back at him, swearing at him, too. He kicked gravel at Burke—then the two big guys lifted Elliot up off the ground by his elbows. Burke said something and they all took off across the courts and across the grass, the big guys hoisting Elliot between them while he twisted and kicked, flailing, trying his hardest to hurt somebody. Burke would dance backward just out of reach of Elliot's kicks, then he'd poke his face in Elliot's to mock and yell and curse at him.

It was crazy.

I ran up to the little weapon on the ground. It was a black sock . . . a little kid's sock. It had something lumpy in it. I picked it up and some marbles fell out onto the gravelly sand. Colored marbles, cat's-eyes. He'd loaded them into one of his socks. He probably got them from his old toy box.

Marbles.

They hauled him onto the bridge. The narrow wood walkway made clacking sounds as Burke hopped backward on it, then it thumped under the bigger guys' heavy feet. They stopped in the middle. The big guys hoisted Elliot up and Burke grabbed his legs and squeezed his ankles together, then pushed them over the railing.

"Hey!" I yelled. I started running. "Hey, *don't*!"

But the two big guys were leaning out and dangling Elliot over the river and the rocks. His feet were flailing around, whacking the wood slats of the bridge. I could hear the water swooshing loudly below. It wasn't a long drop—maybe five or six feet—and it wasn't a very deep river. But it was deep enough, and those were big rocks.

I ran onto the bridge and stopped. They had him over the edge. I didn't know what to do. "Don't," I said. "Don't!"

Burke was leaning over the railing, yelling in Elliot's face.

"Time to say you're sorry, *Geekowitz*!"

Burke's neck looked like it was strung inside with tight wires, and his face was bright red as he yelled, "Say, *I'm sorry, Mister Brown! I shouldn't have done it, Mister Brown!*"

"You suck, Brown! You all suck! You're all ganging-up suckhead coward asses, you know that?"

"Geez—you can't even swear normal, Geekowitz!" said Blanchette, smiling. "So, you want to fly, Bird Boy? Or would you like to apologize to the man?"

Elliot's head whipped around. He spat in Blanchette's face.

I yelled, *"No!"* and sprinted toward them.

Blanchette's head jerked back; his arm shot up to wipe his cheek. Elliot's head dropped, Chris lunged, and then

Blanchette went lunging, too. They tried to grab him, but it was too late. They were leaning down grappling and I got there just as Elliot, his hands grabbing upward and his face wide open, came loose and fell away.

He was crumpled up in the rocks, partway down in the rushing water. Burke and Blanchette backed up and looked at me, wide-eyed. Then they turned and pounded off the bridge.

They were gone.

Chris grabbed my arm. "Come on!" he yelled.

We ran the other way, the bridge shaking beneath us. We scrambled down the steep riverbank, and started hopping across the rocks.

"Elliot!" I was yelling. *"Elliot!"* I couldn't hear an answer.

Out where the water kept them wet the big rocks were slippery. You had to stay on the dry parts or you could go down. Chris jumped ahead, from rock to rock. Out in the middle he put his hand on a rock and hopped down into water. I slipped and banged my knee—but I got there.

Under the bridge Chris was in swirling water up to his waist. He was leaning back against the current and he had Elliot by the shoulders, trying to pull him out of the water. Elliot's head was rolling around.

I slid down and into the water. I guess it was cold; I didn't notice. I got one of Elliot's arms and Chris hauled on the other. We pulled him loose and hoisted him onto a rock. I was yelling at him, the water was rushing by, and my heart was pounding in my ears.

VULCANIZING

"Why?" Catalina said. "Why'd he do it?"

We were sitting in the emergency room on colored plastic chairs, the kind with a shiny square bar underneath the whole row.

"Well, he was mad about what happened to you," I said. "But I also think it was all the stuff people've done to him for years."

"People have really been doing things to him for years?"

"Oh yeah. It's always been open season on Elliot."

She shook her head. Her face was flushed. "And those two just ran away?"

"Yeah. When they lost him and he fell, they got scared."

"They could have killed him."

"Well . . . it wasn't that far to fall."

"But he hit his head."

"Yeah." I couldn't argue with that. When we pulled Elliot out, his eyes were rolling back and he didn't know where he was. He didn't know *who* he was.

Catalina was looking down the hall where they'd taken Elliot. His mom was in there with him. His two older sisters,

Jaimie and Hannah, were looking up at the TV that was hanging in a corner. My mom sat next to them, paging through a magazine.

After we got him out, after Chris ran to the house next to the park and called for the ambulance and came back, I went and called my mom at work. I asked if she would try to find Catalina's number, and call her. The ambulance came, then my mom picked me up and took me home so I could change, then we picked up Catalina and drove to the hospital. Chris didn't come. He was pretty upset. "We didn't mean to," he kept saying while we were waiting for the ambulance. "We didn't mean to."

"Catalina?" My mom was looking up from her magazine. "Do your parents know you're here?"

"I left a note for my dad."

"Oh," she said. "What about your mom?"

Catalina looked away. "She's not here," she said softly. "She's back home."

"Back home?"

"Yes. I am from the Philippines."

My mom looked interested, but you could see she decided to ease up, thank god. She went back to her magazine.

I felt bad. "I'm sorry," I said.

Catalina looked up quickly. "About what?"

I could feel my face heat up. "About . . . you know . . . about what happened. What those girls wrote. That was totally wrong, for them to say that."

She was looking at me. "You think it was true, don't you?"

"No! I mean . . . it doesn't matter."

"What do you mean it doesn't matter?" The mask was gone, that's for sure. She was really upset. She whispered, "What if they told everybody? What if everybody thinks it's true?"

61

"Everybody wouldn't."

"But they don't *know*." She looked around. Nobody else was listening. "You don't know," she whispered.

I thought about that. "I guess that's why they could say it," I said. " 'Cause nobody knows what's really true."

She sat there, staring ahead. "I know it," she said softly. She turned to me. "I know what's true."

"Okay. It's okay."

But of course it wasn't okay, and I knew it wasn't. Why did I keep saying things were okay when nothing was?

Mrs. Gekewicz came out. My mom popped up, and the sisters forgot the TV.

"It's really not that bad," Elliot's mom said. "He's got a minor concussion, an abraded arm, and a badly sprained ankle. The doctor says the worst thing is he'll be on crutches for a couple of weeks. And he may be a little spaced out."

Hannah looked at Jaimie, the older sister, and said, "How will we tell?" But Jaimie frowned.

My mom went over and took Mrs. Gekewicz's hands. Elliot's mom squeezed them, then she came up to me.

"Thank you, Russell," she said. "Thank you. You probably saved his life."

I didn't know what to say. "It wasn't just me," I said, but she had already turned to take Catalina's hand, too. "I wish you could have seen his face when I told him you were here—both of you," she said. "Getting together with you two has made *such* a difference for him."

It has? I thought, Wasn't he better off before? I remembered him paging through those dinosaur books in the library, looking up excitedly to show me stuff before this whole thing started. Then I thought about his little marbles and his little black sock, lying in that gravel.

I got him into this, didn't I? This is just another total screwup by me. This whole, total disaster. It's my fault.

I had to stop this from getting worse. I *had* to. No more stupid experiments. No more pretending we were scientists or something; it was like painting a bull's-eye on our faces, for some reason. Everyone was hurt, and hurt bad. I looked at Catalina. Her expression was complicated.

That's it, I thought. Enough is enough.

"Elliot's family seems nice," Catalina said in the car on the way home. She was sitting up front with my mom.

"It's a good family," my mom said. "His dad travels a lot. But I think they're very close. He's lucky."

I said, "Elliot's lucky?"

My mom glanced at me in the rearview mirror. "Why shouldn't Elliot be lucky?"

"Mom, he gets dumped on by anybody who feels like it, anytime they feel like it."

"I know. But he has people. He has his family. And his mom's right—now he has you two."

I sagged in my seat. Didn't they understand what a disaster this was? Hadn't we just come from a hospital? Hello?

"You mentioned your dad, Catalina," my mom said. "Did you . . . want to come with him to this country?"

Catalina shook her head. "I wanted to stay with my mom. My dad said it was best for me to get an American education."

"You're sure getting one," I said. My mom looked sharply at me in the rearview mirror.

"So," I said to Catalina a little later. "This whole scientific investigation thing. What a boneheaded idea *that* was, huh?"

She blinked. "What do you mean?"

We were at AJ's, a burger-and-ice-cream place, having hot chocolate. I suddenly remembered: The original idea was Catalina's, wasn't it?

"It's not that it was a bad *idea*," I said quickly, "it's just that . . . okay, we tried it. It didn't work, to say the least. We better give it up and find something else to do. Right?"

"But . . . why?"

"Why what?" My mom was sitting down.

"Oh," I said, "we had this idea, but it didn't work out."

"What idea?"

"It's nothing. Really."

"It's *not* nothing," Catalina said. "I don't see why we should give up."

"Give up what?"

"It's really nothing," I told my mom. I turned to Catalina. "Look," I said, pointing at my eye. "See what happened to me? Remember where we just were? See how upset you are?"

"Are you upset, Catalina?"

"*Mom* . . ."

"Okay," she said. "I just wondered . . ."

"Now Elliot can't even walk," I said to Catalina. "Why would we want any more of this?"

"But," she said, "if you're doing an experiment and you don't like your first results . . ."

"It was a disaster. It didn't work."

"It didn't work at *first*," Catalina said. "But that doesn't mean we should just give up."

"Would someone please tell me what in the world you two are talking about?" my mom said.

Catalina told her. "We said we would try to learn things about certain people who were . . . giving us trouble."

"Making our life hell," I said.

Catalina nodded. "So we tried doing some things differently, to see what they'd do. It was an experiment."

"It was nothing."

"It wasn't nothing to me," Catalina said, sitting back and crossing her arms.

"I still want to be *friends*," I said. "I just don't want any more disasters. We're not going to get people to change anyway, so why don't we just let it go?"

"I remember talking about this, the other night," my mom said. "This was how you got punched, wasn't it?"

"Yep. It was idiotic. And it was my fault."

"It wasn't anybody's fault—it was just something we tried," Catalina said. She looked at my mom. "What do scientists do if their experiments don't work?"

I said, "Visit their colleague in the emergency room and then go out for hot chocolate?"

They both ignored me, for some reason.

"Well," my mom said, "*pure* scientists pretty much focus on understanding things. Did you just want to understand these people better, or did you want to change their behavior?"

"Both," Catalina said. "Especially the change."

My mom nodded. She thought for a minute.

"If you're trying to solve a problem and you haven't had good results, you might try some creative thinking," she said. "Try looking at your methods *and* your results differently. What have you tried? What might you try differently? There may be something in there that's waiting for you to notice it, like a hidden key."

Catalina nodded.

"Sometimes that's where the breakthroughs come, the famous ones," my mom said. "Almost by accident, after a whole lot of what seemed like failure. Like the man who first vulcanized rubber."

"Vulcanized rubber?" I said. I mean, come on.

"Sure," my mom said. "It was Charles Goodyear, the man they named the blimp after. Back in the 1800s, raw native rubber was very interesting to people, but not very useful. It was stretchy at normal temperatures, but when it got cold, it turned brittle and broke—and when it got hot, it went soft and melted. Goodyear was an inventor, and he was looking for a way to make rubber stay strong and flexible no matter what happened to it. A lot of other people were trying to do the same thing, but nobody could.

"Everything Goodyear tried, failed. Then one day he was mixing some sulfur and other chemicals into a batch of raw india rubber, and he dropped some on a hot stove. He left it there. The next morning, the stove and the mix on top had cooled down, and it was still rubbery! He'd done it!"

My mom was bright-eyed. She gets excited about strange things.

"Well," she said, "don't you see? Strong and flexible rubber changed the world. Because we had it, people could invent tires and cars and airplanes and all kinds of machinery, along with basketballs and footballs and everything inflatable. Goodyear named his mixing and heating process vulcaniz- ing, and it's still done today. He found it by accident—but the accident happened because he tried. And because he kept trying."

Catalina stood up. "Ms. Trainor," she said, "could you please take me home?"

"Of course, Catalina," my mom said, turning over the check. "Is anything wrong?"

"No. I just want to do something."

"Do what?" I said as we walked toward the door.

"I'll call you later," she said.

"That's an impressive girl," my mom said after we dropped Catalina off. "Very bright and determined. And she's going to be a great beauty."

"She's going to be a *what*?"

My mother gave me her patient smile. It meant, "You men have no clue." I was familiar with it.

"You just wait," she said.

"They call her Olive Oyl."

"Who does?"

"The girls who give her trouble."

"Who's that?"

"Well . . . Bethany DeMere."

"Bethany. Yes, I remember. She's fairly glamorous, isn't she?"

"She thinks so."

My mom sighed. "Girls your age are so easily threatened," she said. "It's a shame."

"You think . . . you think Bethany DeMere is threatened by *Catalina*?"

"I wouldn't be in the least surprised."

"Why?"

"Take a good look at Catalina sometime," my mom said. "Imagine what happens when that long body fills in, and that black hair grows out a little. She has lovely features, and her color—it's beautiful. If I were the reigning glamour queen of your grade, I'd be worried."

I shook my head, trying to clear it. "So you think that's why Bethany's trying to crush her?"

"That would be my strong suspicion," my mom said. "And it's too bad. Girls at this age can be really vicious, and so vulnerable. I almost think it's more serious business than you boys with your physical stuff."

"You think that's worse than being dropped off a bridge? Or punched in the face?"

My mom glanced over at me.

"I'm not saying any of this is easy. But that girl . . . she's in a new country. She doesn't have her mom here. Try to imagine how it must feel to have people in her new school suddenly turn on her."

But I didn't have to imagine it. That part I got.

ROSE

After dinner Catalina called.

"I sent you a message," she said.

"All right."

A pause.

"I'm not sure what to do with it," she said.

"Why?"

Another pause.

"You'll see," she said finally. "Tell me what you think . . . but wait till tomorrow. In school. Okay?" She sounded nervous.

"Well, okay. Sure."

I got on-line. Catalina's message just said, "Please read this. I thought it was a good idea before. Now I don't know."

KidNet downloaded the file she had attached to the message. I opened it. Here's what it said:

For some reason, sometimes when you are new or different in some way, people decide to tell lies about you. I don't know why. Before I came to Parkland School I didn't know people did that at all.

My name is Catalina Aarons. I'm somebody people have been telling untrue things about. Maybe you have heard some things. In fact, if you are in seventh grade and you have heard anything about me, it's probably not true. I haven't really told people what is true, so maybe in a way it's partly my fault.

So here are some things about me that are true.

I was born in the Philippines, on the biggest island, Luzon. My mother is a Filipina. My father is American. His company sent him to work in Manila, the capital city, and that's where he met my mom. They got married, and they had me. So I am half-Filipina and half-American.

Filipinos are a mix of types of people, just like Americans. Our ancestors include the people of our part of the Pacific, called Malays, and Chinese people, and also Spanish and Americans, because both of those countries used to control the Philippines. My mother's name is Rosario. That's Spanish. But everyone calls her by her American nickname, Rose.

We lived near Manila but not right in it, in a house not that much different from the houses here. My dad went to work. He was gone a lot. My mom and I were best friends. My mom is really beautiful. Everyone said so! She is not as tall as me and she looks like a Spanish princess, with dark eyes, and she has long shining black hair like a Malay, and her eyes are almond-shaped like the Chinese. People used to tell me she got the best of everything.

My mom teaches music, mostly piano but also singing, to kids and grownups who come to our home. She used to sing to me, since I was a baby. Her voice is like liquid silver.

I rode to school and came home every day on a jeepney. That's like an American school bus only it isn't—it's a funny decorated contraption made from adding almost anything onto an old American jeep, or a small truck. There are jeepneys all over Manila. Some of them are incredible!

Anyway, every day when the jeepney let me off after school I ran home, because my mom and I would have *merienda*.

Merienda is an afternoon snack. It's not like any American snack. We might have *adobo*, which is chicken or meat cooked in an incredible sauce—I can't even describe how it tasted, tangy and just a little sweet. My mom would make *panyo panyo*, little pastries filled with banana and mango jam. They are fantastic! We'd have *guapple* pie, too. Guapple is a kind of hard fruit, like an apple but sweeter and softer in its taste. We'd have slices of mango with lime juice dripped over them, and hot chocolate whipped up smooth and frothy. And we'd have our own kind of limeade, which was incredible! My mom made it from our little *calamansi* limes, mixed up with melon juice and water.

Every day my mom made *merienda* for her and me, and we would talk about everything. Everything! We were happy. But I guess my dad was not. I guess he missed America, and he did not like being a foreigner in Luzon. I guess he had some problems with my mom's family. (He was the only one who was not Filipino.) When he was home he didn't seem happy, and then my mom started to cry a lot. I would hear her playing the piano and crying. I didn't really know what was wrong.

One day they told me they were going to get a divorce, and I would be moving with my dad to America. My dad said I would get a much better education in America. He said I could go home every summer, to be with my mom. He said the schools are so much better here, and the opportunities are so much more. That is what he said.

My mom did not want me to go. But she said my dad was probably right. I won't tell you much about what it was like to leave my home and my family and my school, and especially my mom.

I don't know about the opportunities in America, but so

far I don't think very much of the schools. At least not this school. It's not so much the school—the school is okay, I guess. It's the way some kids treat you in it.

It's funny, in a way. Kids who want to hurt other kids treat them like they are not a human being, but at the same time they figure out the one thing that can hurt you most, as a human being. Like if you are new they make up terrible things about who they say you are, and what you're like, and your family, especially your mom.

I would like people to know that I am proud of where I come from, and I am proud of my family. I am proud of who I am. I don't tell lies either.

You don't have to like me if you don't want to. You don't have to include me or invite me to anything at all if you don't want to. I don't mind. I am making friends. But I don't like it when people get together to act like I am not a person.

So now you know a little bit about me. I guess how you act is up to you.

Catalina Aarons

SYSTEM SERVER

✱The next morning I brought Catalina's letter to school on a disk. When she saw me coming, she hugged her books to her chest and closed her locker slowly.

I walked up fast. "It's incredible," I said.

"It is?"

"Yeah! And you know what? This is the thing to do. It kicks the legs out from under the evil princess."

"The who?"

"You know." I lifted my chin and shook my head, as if rippling my golden tresses.

"Oh, yes." She nodded. "I got the idea from you."

"Huh?"

"Elliot said you wrote down what happened. When that boy hit you."

"Oh. I forgot I did that."

"Well, I didn't."

The bell rang. We started walking down the hall. "Anyway," I said, "I brought it with me, what you wrote." I lifted the disk out of my shirt pocket.

"I don't know what to do with it," she said. "I mean, what if I did want people to read it? How would I do that?"

"Well, we could print it out. You know, post it."

"Post it? You mean like on bulletin boards?" She shuddered. "That would be totally humiliating."

"Well . . . we could give it to certain people. Like a letter."

"You mean *those* people? Slip it into their lockers the way they do to me? What do you think they'd do with it?"

"I don't know."

"They'd ignore it. Or they'd laugh about it. And nobody else would know the difference."

"I guess."

We were almost to Ms. Hogeboom's social studies class. The door was open and kids were slipping in around us. We hung back.

"What else could we do?" she whispered.

"I don't know."

"Think more about it."

I said, "Can I send it to Elliot? He might have some ideas."

The second bell rang. She nodded as she turned, took a deep breath, and stepped into class. I went in, too.

In activities block I signed into the computer lab so I could send a message to Elliot at home. The room was full, as usual. Kids sat at computers around the walls and at the back-to-back line of them down the center of the room. Everyone was plugged in, tapping at keys, slouched back or tilting forward to peer at screens. I found an empty station, sat down, and clicked up KidNet.

Mostly kids use KidNet to send messages to each other, but as I've said we can also send messages to teachers, which is useful if you're confused about some homework or you don't understand something or you forgot which chapters to study for a test.

There are three levels of access. They're controlled by Mr. Dallas, the computer lab teacher and network administrator. The highest level, Staff, is for the teachers and administration. The second is MidStream, which everyone else has. This access can be suspended, or revoked, if you misuse it or behave badly on the system. Kids tend to be fairly careful about that because nobody wants to lose messaging privileges. We're always checking our messages.

Because KidNet is a local area network, it's self-contained. That means it's all ours, and it's only us. We can access the Internet, also, from most school machines, though there's safeguard software so you can't download anything pornographic or even write swear words in an Internet message. But on KidNet we can pretty much say whatever we want. There's no censorship, and also all the Net weirdos and the people selling stuff can't get at us. You can't get into KidNet from outside unless Mr. Dallas lets you.

The third access level is just Library. That's what you don't want. You can call up encyclopedias, CD-ROMs, and other research stuff, but you can't send messages or anything. If you lose MidStream access, you're stuck in this cyber-punishment ghetto, where you can only find stuff they want you to learn. Obviously, nobody wants that.

I tapped out a message for Elliot. I slipped my disk into the drive and attached Catalina's file from the disk to the message. Elliot had nothing much else to do at home, so as I did some other stuff I wasn't surprised to see a response pop up pretty quickly.

<TROO> This is perfect!
<RUSST> Yes.
<TROO> Everyone should see it.
<RUSST> Yes but how?
<TROO> Ask Mr. D. How's school? Seen Richie?

<RUSST> Saw him today. He didn't look at me. School's OK. You're not missing much.

<TROO> This is boring though.

<RUSST> I got to go. Five minutes left in block.

<TROO> Ask Mr. D!

Right as I signed off, the bell rang. Machines beeped and chairs scraped as people signed off, got up, grabbed their backpacks, and crowded through the door. I sat there watching. Finally I got up, walked to the door . . . and turned back.

I looked at the machines. They were waiting for the next wave. I thought how "Ask Mr. D" came pecking across my screen as Elliot typed it. And then I knew.

Of course!

"I have an idea," I told Catalina when school ended. "Come with me, okay?"

"Okay."

I took off walking. Her locker clicked shut; in about three seconds she had caught up and was striding alongside me.

I looked at her. "Some legs," I said.

She blushed.

"I mean they're *long*," I said, embarrassed. She blushed even more. I managed not to embarrass us any more before we got to the System Server room.

That's what it says on the door: SYSTEM SERVER. This was always the first place to look for Mr. Dallas. I knocked.

"Come ON in!" said a booming voice. I pushed open the door. Inside, Mr. Dallas swiveled his chair toward us from a blinking screen.

The headquarters of SchoolStream is no bigger than a closet, which is what it was before this year, when they put in the network. There are no windows. Tall metal racks, looking like they're from grownup erector sets, hold electronic equipment in shelves almost to the ceiling. At desk level are four or five computers.

"RussT! Catli! How are ya?"

Mr. Dallas is a funny guy, mostly in the humorous sense. He likes to call you by your screen name, and he always shakes your hand with gusto. He has a lot of gusto. He rides a motorcycle to work, and he has a crop of gray hair that's so thick and stiff it looks like he hit a porcupine and it stuck to his head.

Catalina blinked and sort of smiled at Mr. Dallas. I don't think she had experienced him up close before.

KidNet is Mr. Dallas's baby. He convinced the school to put it in and let him run it. Before this year he taught science; now he's always bounding into other teachers' science classes to give a talk on KidNet, answer questions, and urge us to use it, which he doesn't have to do, since everyone started using it right away. Mr. Dallas says we're *innovators*.

"What can I do for you guys?"

"We've got a KidNet question, Mr. D."

"I *love* it. Sit down, sit down." We sat. He said, "What is it?"

I said, "Catalina's written something." I pulled the disk out of my pocket.

"It's a letter," she said, perching on a swivel chair. "I'd like to send it to everyone in the seventh grade."

"Is that possible on KidNet?" I said. "Can we do that?"

"Sure! The easiest way is to attach the file to an e-mail message and send it to a distribution list. That's the network version of a mailing list. In fact, distribution lists go back to the earliest computer networks, when the U.S. government set one up in case of nuclear attack. Users on the network created a mailing list so they could talk about science fiction."

He leaned back, hands behind his head, and chuckled.

"Imagine some far-flung network of computer nerds holed up in basement labs and bomb shelters after an atomic holocaust, with everyone on-line intently debating some science-fiction story about life after an atomic holocaust." He looked at us and grinned. "Doesn't that just say it all?"

I wasn't sure what all it said, but Mr. Dallas broke out laughing. Catalina and I looked at each other. He suddenly sat up in his chair. "So," he said, swiveling to a computer, "we have a number of automated lists. Teachers use them all the time. You're the first students to ask about them."

He started rattling keys . . . then he paused.

"There *could* be some pitfalls here," he said.

"There could?"

"Well, possibly. I mean, if students start to get the idea about distributing or broadcasting files . . . it opens up a new dimension of use. It could be a Pandora's box. That's . . . well, actually, that's what certain authority figures darkly predicted this whole network would become."

Catalina said, "They did?"

"Well, yes. There were people in positions of authority—one person, basically—who said if we turned a LAN over to the students as an open system, we'd get chaos. Of course, we *don't* have chaos—we have use. But I wonder what'll happen if you start broadcasting files."

"It'd be innovative," I quickly said.

"Yeah! It sure would. Well, I'm for it." He grinned at us again. "Experimentation, communication—that's what this is about, right?"

Now he lunged forward; his chair almost leaped at us. Catalina hopped backward in hers.

"It *is* important for you to be careful with this," Mr. Dallas said. "Okay?"

Catalina gripped her armrests. "Okay," she said, wide-eyed.

"How should we be careful?" I asked.

"Just don't do anything irresponsible," Mr. Dallas said. "But I know you won't. Anyway, what you do is pull down this menu and choose Distribute. See it? First you've created your message. Then, let's see—Staff access gets you all the lists we've created. What does MidStream access get?"

He rattled some keys. The list choices that popped up said Grade 6, Grade 7, Grade 8, All, and Custom. There were other list names, like Hogeboom 7B, but they were in faded gray, meaning you couldn't use them at our access level.

"Okay. I thought so," Mr. Dallas said. "You can access what you need. You could create custom lists of your own, if you wanted to. But you just want to send it to Grade 7, right? So, no problem. Just select that and send."

"All right," I whispered. I slipped the disk with Catalina's letter back in my pocket.

"I guess we'll go try it," I said.

Mr. Dallas shook our hands with gusto.

"Onward!" he said.

That night I rode my bike to Elliot's house. I had never been there before.

He said, "You know what I can't stand?"

I didn't answer. I was looking around at his bedroom.

Elliot was sitting on his bed, his thickly wrapped ankle propped up on a big yellow pillow. The pillow was, as far as I could tell, the only non-dinosaur-themed item in the room.

His walls had posters from the original *Godzilla* movie ("King of the Monsters!"), plus *Godzilla vs. Mothra* and *One Million Years B.C.* (which didn't actually feature dinosaurs so much as this starlet in skins, with major cleavage), plus pictures of stegosaurus and iguanodon and triceratops and a very wide-angle poster that showed a ferny river scene with volcanoes spouting smoke in the background, tyrannosaurus blasting out of the foliage to attack some panicking duck-bills, and a giant brontosaurus off munching in the water. On the shelves he had a battery-powered triceratops, a wooden giant flying lizard skeleton, a plastic dueling tyranno and triceratops, at least thirty realistic little rubber or plastic dino models, a dinosaur diorama, and a webbed dino foot-print in plaster.

And he had a bookshelf full of dinosaur books. A chubby, inflated green T-rex was tipped over backward in the corner. On Elliot's bed was a dinosaur comforter—it had a red duckbill, a blue bronto, a green pterodactyl, a yellow tyranno. They were all smiling. I said that didn't seem too realistic, dinos smiling.

"Nah," Elliot said, waving it away, "I got all this stuff when I was a kid. You know what I can't stand? I'm stuck here and those guys think they won. They probably think, 'Hey, man, we showed *him*,' and I can't do anything about it." He lifted his wrapped foot a little, then let it drop.

"Pretty soon, though," he said, "it's my turn." He started to smile, slyly.

"What, are you nuts? They dropped you off a bridge."

"Yeah. And you know what? I am going to get them back."

I thought, Who is this kid? What happened to the cautious little Bird Boy? Elliot was sitting up proudly, with his arms crossed.

I sighed. "Well, we need to change our approach," I said. "There's no future in getting the crap beat out of us."

"Maybe not," he said. "But I stood up to 'em, didn't I? Just like you did. They might think twice before harassing *me* again."

"Yeah. They think you're insane."

"You think so? They think I'm nuts?"

"You *were* nuts. Totally."

"Yeah." He was just beaming. I shrugged. Maybe he *was* a little nuts. Maybe the concussion . . .

"Hey," I said. "Has anybody talked to you or anything? Like the principal or the police?"

"Nah," he said. "Forget about the principal—I told you, she never does anything. The cops . . . my mom wanted to make a report but I said don't. Burke and Blanchette would say they were trying to save me or something. The worst kids are the best liars." He shrugged. "So what."

"If it was grownups who did that, they'd be in jail."

"Well it wasn't and they're not. Hey, what'd you do with Catalina's thing?"

I told him we'd sent it around to the whole seventh grade. We'd gone right from the System Server room to the computer lab, and done it.

Elliot whistled. "I like it! Hey, can you believe those girls made that stuff up, about Catalina and her mom?"

"I told you they did."

"Yeah. What do you think people will say? I mean when they read what she wrote?"

"I don't know. They'll *read* it. Most of 'em probably already did. And I bet they'll talk about it. I just don't know what they'll say."

"Tell me what happens, okay?"

"Yeah. I'll make a report."

"A lab report," Elliot said, and he smiled again. "The bully lab lives."

SOCIAL STUDIES

The next day in social studies we were doing *Anne Frank*. We were halfway through the book. Ms. Hogeboom said, "People, let's talk today about Anne as a person. What was she like, do you think?"

The usual heavy silence. Answers came like questions.

"She was bright?"

"She was a prolific writer?"

"Well, yes," Ms. Hogeboom said. "But do you think she was annoying?"

"Huh?"

"What do you mean, *annoying*?"

"Well, Anne writes again and again that she is the center of all the tension in the Secret Annex," the teacher said, perching on her desk and picking up the paperback from beside her.

Ms. Hogeboom has long straight hair and she wears long, loose, peasant kind of dresses. I think she used to be a hippie. Her copy of the book had a lot of bent yellow Post-its sticking up from the top, like a shaggy blond Mohawk. She pulled one of the yellow tabs open to a page.

"How about this? On page 29 she says, 'Nothing, I repeat, nothing about me is right; my general appearance, my character, my manners are discussed from A to Z.' Then she says, 'Am I really so bad-mannered, conceited, headstrong, pushing, stupid, lazy, etc., etc., as they all say?' "

Ms. Hogeboom looked up. "What do you think? Was she?"

There was buzzing and murmuring now.

"People always say that about teenagers."

"Yeah. It's ridiculous."

"It's *stupid*."

"All right. So is she just a normal adolescent who is being typically persecuted and misunderstood? I mean, everyone who's hiding together in that little apartment has to be pretty edgy, right? Maybe they just take it out on Anne, who could really be the nicest teenage person in the world. Anne Frank has become a hero in our eyes, and for good reason. *But* . . . is it at all possible that as a person, at this time in her life, she might have been a little bit exasperating? What if you'd been stuck with her in that apartment? What do you think she was really like?"

There was a lot of murmuring now. Some people were flipping through their copies; some were rolling their eyes, making faces, and whispering to their friends. When you ask seventh graders to share anything, you always get a certain amount of that.

"She was very intelligent," Leah Sternberg piped up helpfully. Leah talks a lot, always helpfully. She's involved with everything—Student Council, school newspaper, drama club, soccer and basketball and softball, chorus *and* band . . . Whenever there's an awkward moment in class, Leah will pipe up.

"She was also very sensitive," she added.

"She was *hyper*sensitive," said Jake Messner. Jake's a tall kid who's good in sports and very smart and serious. He's actually one of the nicer kids in our class. "She says so herself," he said. "It's in here somewhere." He was searching through pages, frowning.

"She does say she's hypersensitive," Ms. Hogeboom agreed, and opened her book, too.

"Well, for god's sake," said Allison Kukovna, "who *wouldn't* be? I mean, she's very bright and she's got all these interests in life, she loves her friends and she even likes school, and now she's shut up all day and all night with her parents and these other dorky grownups she doesn't even *know* who can't tell each other they really hate each other so they pick apart everything Anne does. And, I mean, if any of them makes one loud noise they could all be *dead*. Wouldn't you be a little edgy?"

Allison shut her book with a thump. "It's not fair to say it's Anne's fault." She crossed her arms and sat up straight, dramatically.

Allison has cascading red hair and she is dramatic. She sang the lead when the chorus and band did a number from *Annie* in the last school concert. She was funny and good. She could be one of the cool girls, except I think she's not tense enough.

"It's being stuck in there," Jake said. "They're in those rooms all the time, surrounded by all that fear and danger. It brings out the worst in everybody. I mean, in the beginning she says her family never quarrels—they're shocked when the other family does. But before long everybody is squabbling like crazy."

Ms. Hogeboom smiled. "Anne's got a strong character and she *is* a teenager. So whenever things get edgy, she's a magnet for adult disapproval. Is that what you're saying? People? Is that really what this is about?"

"It's about what it's always about," said a voice in back.

Everybody turned around.

Turner White always sat in the back, and always wore black. He was sort of pale, like he didn't get a lot of sun.

"Turner?" Ms. Hogeboom said. "What is it always about?"

Turner shrugged. "Isolation," he said. "What else?"

We just looked at him.

"Well?" he said. "If it wasn't for the isolation, none of this would have happened."

"*None* of it?" Ms. Hogeboom said.

Turner tilted his head like he was waiting for the rest of us to get it. "Think about it," he said. "The Nazis take over all of Europe and they isolate it, right? Nobody can go in or out. They hate the Jews, so they isolate them. Right? It says in the book no Jews were allowed to visit Christians or go to the movies or the parks or anything. Right? Then they start shipping people off to those camps, where they're completely cut off. And meanwhile these two families have to hide upstairs in a warehouse with blankets over the windows."

Turner sat back and folded his arms. "If it wasn't for the isolation, none of this *could* have happened."

There was a silence.

"Well," said Leah helpfully, "what if the Jewish people had a computer network? I mean, what if the Franks could have sent messages?"

Somebody said, *"What?"*

"Well, why not? All over the world. 'We're in here. We're hiding. They're trying to *kill* us. Please help.'"

"Then the Germans would have found them and killed them a lot sooner," said Jon Blanchette. He twisted around, shrugged, and grinned. "Well?"

"It's a big joke to you, isn't it, Jon?" said Big Chris, turning to face his friend. "Nothing but a big joke—no matter who gets hurt."

Jon gave him a funny look, and shrugged.

"But," said Allison, "what if you could send messages when people *started* to tell lies about you?"

"Yeah," said Jake. He leaned forward with a sly expression. "What if you could tell everyone the truth about yourself right away?"

People were shifting in their seats and sneaking glances at Catalina, who sat in the middle of the class blinking behind her glasses. Bethany DeMere sat stiffly in the front row. She didn't look around.

Ms. Hogeboom was puzzled. "Well . . ." she said, "Anne was sending a message, wasn't she? Her book has been read by millions of people."

"But she's dead," I said.

Everyone looked at me.

"Well, she is. What good did writing the book do her?"

"It's a good question," Ms. Hogeboom said. "What do you all think . . ."

"But what if she could have sent messages to everyone when this whole thing started?" Allison said. "What if they *all* could have?"

Ms. Hogeboom said, "What do you mean by . . ."

I said, "The world didn't believe this stuff was happening at all, right? 'Cause the world didn't want to know. Sounds kind of familiar."

"It's true," Allison said. "I mean, if a few people persecute somebody, most of us pretend it isn't happening, right? We don't want to see it. But what if the person it's actually happening to could send a message to everyone, like, right away?"

"What is all this about messages?" Ms. Hogeboom asked.

Everyone knew. Nobody said.

"If Anne Frank had had the Internet," the teacher said

slowly, "she'd be alive today? Is that what you're saying? Anyone?"

"That's pretty stupid," said Burke Brown.

"Well, I don't know," said Jake. "I mean, it all started with lies, right? They pretended the Jewish people were evil. They told everybody they were, and they kept saying it and saying it until everybody at least *acted* like it was true. And meanwhile they were pushing them around, shoving them and locking them up and beating up anybody who disagreed with them."

"It was like the bullies were taking over the world," I said.

"I think that's exactly what it was," said Ms. Hogeboom.

"But," said Jake, "if there had been an Internet then, the Nazis couldn't have stopped it, right? There's, like, sixteen zillion sites on the Web. You can't censor it."

"Yeah," said Blanchette, "but who would have paid attention to just one site?"

"If it was talking about mass *murder*? Hello?"

Everyone started talking at once. Ms. Hogeboom's class got that way sometimes. She wasn't big on control.

Catalina lifted her hand. Everybody got quiet.

"Catalina? Yes?"

She didn't stand up this time. And there were no giggles.

"Anne Frank's whole diary was in one little red-checked writing book," Catalina said quietly. "They found it in a mess of things the Gestapo left on the floor after they took the people away. It wasn't that different from the notebooks we use—not really." She held up her spiral notebook.

"Yes?" Ms. Hogeboom said.

Catalina blinked. "That's all," she said. "Anne Frank wasn't trying to stop anything, or change anyone. She was just writing down her story."

The bell rang but nobody moved. Ms. Hogeboom was

nodding and looking around, looking pleased, which was funny, because she was the only one who had no idea what anyone was really talking about.

"Okay, everyone, that was excellent," Ms. Hogeboom said. "Now we've run a little late, but for next time, please read through page 175."

Chairs scraped and backpacks zipped.

"Wait," said Turner in the back. The scraping and zipping stopped. "I found it," he said. "Just listen, okay?

" 'Lately I have begun to feel deserted,' " Turner read. " 'I am surrounded by too great a void. I never used to feel like this, my fun and amusements, and my girl friends, completely filled my thoughts. Now I either think about unhappy things, or about myself.' "

The next class was waiting outside. You could see the dark bodies through the frosted glass by the door.

"That's how it is," Turner said. "*That*'s why everyone relates to this kid. It's not because of Nazis, it's 'cause of the blankets on the windows. It's because everyone knows about feeling alone."

After a second, everybody got up and started moving for the door. But nobody spoke. The door opened, and the kids from the next class stepped back and just looked at all these quiet solemn faces filing past.

At lunch I was going for our table in the Bun Appetit corner; but I stopped just past the cash register and stood there, holding my tray. Three girls, Allison Kukovna and two of her friends, were sitting with Catalina, talking with her, at our table. Catalina looked a little bewildered.

I knew it was a good thing, what Catalina did, writing down her story, and then us sending it out. It seemed like it had really hit people. I remembered what my mom said, that Catalina would be beautiful someday. I guessed she had new friends now. And, I mean, if you have new friends, fairly cool friends, who'd want to hang around with two invisible rejects anymore?

Actually, make that one invisible reject.

I realized, standing there, that I had no place to go.

RADIO FREE GEEKOWITZ

✱"Oh, yeah, people read it," I said on the phone. "Nobody actually talked about it directly, at least not that I heard. But they were definitely affected by it. You could tell."

"How?"

"Well . . . the way people acted toward her was a little different. In the lunchroom, Allison Kukovna and her friends went to our table and sat with her."

"They sat at *our* table? What did they say?"

"How should I know? You think I sat there? Anyway, there was this thing in social studies. We were talking about Anne Frank, but then it was like everybody was talking about Catalina at the same time."

"They were? How?"

"Well, it was like they were saying Anne Frank and Catalina were similar, only Catalina had KidNet. Except they didn't mention KidNet exactly."

"They were saying Catalina was like *Anne Frank*?"

"Well . . . kind of."

After a second, Elliot said, "Does that seem a little farfetched to you?"

"Well, now it does, but it made sense at the time. We were talking about how people get persecuted, and that all Anne Frank did was tell her story, and if she'd only had the Internet then maybe things would have been different. 'Cause people would have heard her story right away."

"Huh."

"See, nobody mentioned Catalina by name. But it was like everybody was really talking about her."

"Yeah?"

"Kind of."

"Huh. So how *did* you send that message out, exactly?"

I told him how to find the mailing lists, how to distribute a file. "I'm going to try it," he said.

"With what?"

"I'm not sure. You'll see. Hey, why not? I'm sitting here with nothing else to do."

"Well," I said, "be careful."

"Be *careful*? Of what?"

"I'm not sure, exactly. Mr. Dallas said to be careful."

"All I've ever been is careful," Elliot said. "I'm sick and tired of careful."

After dinner I checked the Net. There was a message from Elliot.

Dear Seventh Grade,
    This is another true story from your Darkland School. Did you read the story of Catalina Aarons? Well, that was from the Bully Lab. And so is this. If you wonder what the Bully Lab is, then good. By the way, this is what happened to me.
    There are three guys . . . You guys know who you are. (Maybe I should tell everyone who you are, guys. What do you think? Should I?) I call these wonderful guys the Jock Rots. Yeah, the Jock Rots, because they're a fungus. They

pick on certain kids because they think it's fantastically funny. Here's what they did to me most recently. You tell me how funny it was.

First they surrounded me after school in front of the School Street park. That was pretty typical. They figured on playing their usual games, like taking things out of my backpack, tearing up my homework sheets, playing keepaway with my library books. I always used to say, "Come on, come on, cut it out, give it back!" And of course they'd laugh and laugh because it was SO funny.

That's what I USED to do. This time I got pissed off. I hit back, and I also told them what I thought of them, and that REALLY upset the poor little boys.

So they picked me up and carried me (it took three of them—I got in every kick and insult I could) to the bridge over the river and they held me over the edge trying to scare me and make me say I was sorry for upsetting their delicate feelings. I didn't say it because I wasn't and AM not. I kept putting up a fight and finally, "accidentally," they dropped me. Off the bridge. On the rocks. In the river.

THEN you know what they did? They ran away.

Isn't that brave? I was down in the water and they took off. My friend had to rescue me and get me to the hospital. I had a concussion and a sprained ankle. But hey, guys, guess what? I'm still here! What are you going to do NOW?

I think people ought to realize that stuff like this goes on every single day at Darkland School. The rest of you are all part of it—because you let it go on and maybe you think it's funny, or you think it only happens to geeky outsiders and kids who are smaller or fatter or skinnier or don't have so many friends or so much money as you. So tell me—what happens when you don't have so many friends one day, or you don't have so much money, or something bad happens to you?

Guess what? It can happen fast. One day you fall just a

little bit behind the crowd, and the next day you can be on the other side. Yes, you too. Falling off a bridge.

Think about it.

Yes, there is a Bully Lab. We are interested in people's true stories of Darkland School. These are ours. What are yours?

Oh, and hey, Jock Rots. I'm not the only one who knows who you are. Sleep tight!

Elliot Gekewicz
The Bully Lab

It wasn't long before Elliot called.

"Well? Did you read it?"

"Yeah. Did you send it to everybody?"

"The whole seventh grade." He was hyped up. "What do you think?"

I sighed. "I don't know. You didn't really tell the whole story, you know."

"You don't think that's the real story?"

"Well, maybe, but . . . saying all those things about those guys . . . I don't know, Elliot. Didn't I tell you it was mainly Chris who pulled you out of the water?"

"You might have mentioned it, but so what? It was him and Blanchette that dropped me in there."

"I don't think they meant to."

"Hey," he said, "whose side are you on? You know the things those guys did to me, all those times before. They never cared how I felt about any of it. So let *them* worry about what happens next. Let them wake up in the morning feeling scared. It's about time they found out what that's like."

"But what happens when you come back, Elliot?"

"I don't know. But what can they do to me that they haven't already done? Besides"—his voice dropped a little—"if I can do *this*, I bet you they won't even try."

"Well, maybe, but you say we're the Bully Lab now. You said Catalina's thing was from the Bully Lab."

"Yeah! It's a good name."

"Well, maybe, but we didn't talk about it. And I'm not so sure Catalina wants to be involved."

"Why?"

"I think she's got new friends now."

There was a long silence.

"Would you call her?" he said. "To find out?"

"I don't know."

"Come on. At least just tell her what I did. Maybe you can find out a little."

"All right. I'll try."

"Let me know," he said.

I sighed. "What am I, your spy?"

"Yeah, man. I'm stuck here."

It was funny, how Elliot was more scared of losing Catalina than of getting stomped by the Jock Rots. But I figured it made sense, somehow, at least to him.

I called her.

"Elliot wrote a thing about what those guys did to him," I said. "He's already sent it out. On KidNet."

"To who?"

"The seventh grade."

"Hmm. Is that good or bad?"

"I'm not sure. It's a pretty feisty letter. I'm kind of afraid it might get us into some trouble."

"Why us?"

"Elliot says we're the Bully Lab. In his letter, I mean. He says your letter came from the Bully Lab, just like his."

"My letter came from me," Catalina said.

"I know. And, you know . . . I mean, I figure you probably won't want to hang out with us anymore anyway. You know."

After a second, she said, "What are you talking about?"

"Well, I saw you having lunch with Allison and her friends."

"So?"

"So I guess you have new friends now."

"I don't understand," she said. "I wrote something, and I'm glad people read it. I'm glad those girls wanted to say they liked it. But it doesn't change who I am. It doesn't change who my friends are."

"It doesn't?"

"No."

"But what if those girls start to be your friends?"

"What if they do? Why should that change anything?"

"I just figured it would."

"Well, I don't," she said.

The next afternoon in activities block I checked my e-mail. I had something from Elliot.

You and Catalina better come to my house after school, OK?
There's some stuff here you should see.

Catalina had a saxophone lesson after school. I told her how to get to Elliot's, and she said she'd meet us there.

After school I was walking past the park. Burke and Blanchette were on the basketball court, shooting. Big Chris wasn't with them. I wasn't seeing Big Chris with them at all anymore, come to think of it.

I kept walking. Burke and Blanchette stopped playing. They came out on the street.

"Russ T, my man," Blanchette said. He flashed me his golden-boy grin. Burke was behind him, not smiling.

"Hey, man," Blanchette said, "what's up with that friend of yours?"

"Why? You guys worried about something?"

Burke stepped around Blanchette; he stuck his sharp angry face up to mine. "Hey, kid—it's your little geek friend who needs to worry."

"You think so? Really?"

Blanchette pulled Burke aside. "I told you I'd talk to him," I heard him whisper.

"Yeah, well you *talk* to him," Burke whispered back. His eyes flashed over Blanchette's shoulder at me. "You tell him."

"Okay," Blanchette whispered. "Be cool."

He turned back and spread his hands, like this was no big deal.

"We're just concerned that your friend is suddenly broadcasting some pretty wild stories," he said.

"Yeah," Burke growled. "Radio Free Geekowitz."

"It's true," I said. "I know it's true, and you know I know. I saw it."

"Yeah, well it doesn't matter what *you* saw," Burke said, stepping around Blanchette and getting in my face again. "It doesn't mean a thing what *you* saw."

"No? How do you figure that, Burke?" I had been face to face with Richie Tucker. This was nothing.

Burke turned deep red. He was actually shaking.

"Look," Blanchette said, smiling as he drew Burke aside again. "You were there," he said to me. "Elliot exaggerated, right? It was an accident, what happened. It was his fault as much as anyone's! You saw what he did to us."

"What he did to *you*? Like what, finally trying to hit back, after all the crap you've done to him?"

Blanchette's smile got bigger. "Yeah." He chuckled. "I mean, we were shocked. We always figured we were just playing around together. He always seemed to like the attention. You know?"

I stepped back. "Jon," I said, "just how stupid do you think I am?"

"Listen, you little zit," Burke spat out, stepping into my face a third time. "You go ahead and think you're the smartest little zit in the world, okay? You and your little zit friend go play with your computers all you want, okay? But you tell your zit friend, *No names.* You tell him that, okay? *No names!*"

He shoved me. "If he broadcasts anything with our names in it, I will personally . . ."

"You will personally what?"

We all looked around. Richie Tucker stepped out from the woods behind the tennis courts. He started coming toward us.

"You will personally what?" he said, walking up to Burke. He raised his eyebrows. "Hmm?"

"Nothing," Burke said, turning away.

"Hey, Richie," Blanchette said. "What's up, man?"

"That's what I wonder," Richie said. He tapped his chin with one finger. "I see two guys pushing one kid around. I'm thinking, Is this a fight? It looks like a fight. Looks like fun. Two against one. I'm thinking it would be even more fun if it was . . . two against two."

Burke and Blanchette were already backing away. "You remember what I said," Burke said to me, not looking at Richie.

I grinned. Burke's face clenched up, then he glanced at Richie. He turned around and started walking away.

"We'll see you guys later," Blanchette said, smiling.

Richie and I watched them go.

They left their ball.

"What was *that* about?" Richie said.

So I told him. "Those two dropped my friend off that

bridge. My friend had to go to the hospital, and he's still not back in school. He got mad. So he told the story of what happened and broadcast it to the whole seventh grade."

"What, on the radio?"

"On KidNet."

"You can do that?"

"We found out you can," I said. "But Elliot, that's my friend, he didn't tell people those guys' names. Now they're worried he'll tell. They're trying to scare us."

Richie looked at the Rots, walking down School Street. Blanchette glanced back at us. Richie snorted.

"They're squids," he said.

I grinned. "Yeah."

"They got nothing."

"Naw." I looked at him. "You know, you didn't have to do that."

"Look, kid, here's how it is. You disrespect me, you pay. You piss me off, you get hurt. Okay? You understand that, we'll do all right. All right?"

I blinked. It took me a second to realize he was talking about punching me.

"Um . . . I didn't mean about that," I said. "I meant just now—with those two. You didn't have to."

"Have to what? Two guys acting like they're going to take you down? Just one of you? Hey, fair is fair."

I shrugged. "Well, thanks."

"Whatever. Hey, you know what? You stood up to those two."

"I did?"

He shrugged. "Not bad."

"Well . . . thanks."

He shoved his hands in his jacket.

"You stood up to me, too," he said.

"What?"

He shrugged. "You asked me those questions. Remember?"

"Yeah . . ."

"It was okay, you asking me those questions," he said quickly. "I mean, I didn't mind it."

"You seemed to mind it," I mumbled. "You hit me."

"Well . . . you just got to ask the right questions."

I said, "Huh." I had no idea what was going on. As usual.

"It's all right," Richie said. "Stand up to people, you get respect. And . . . listen, kid. If you want to ask me questions again sometime, it's okay. You can."

I had no idea what to say. Richie picked up the basketball and handed it to me.

"Here," he said. "Hold on to your balls."

"Oh, it's not mine. You need one?"

His eyebrows clenched and he got in my face. "What are you saying? Are you saying something?"

"What? No!"

He scrutinized me. "You better not be."

I blinked. "I don't know what anybody's talking about," I said.

Richie drew back. "Sure you do," he said. He kept on studying me. But I don't think he was looking for weakness this time.

"Put the squids in their place," he said. "You get that, right?"

I nodded.

"Well," he said, "what else is there?"

I shrugged. "I'm not sure."

"Well, you figure it out," he said. "I'm watching you."

"I know."

Richie looked me in the eye, and nodded. Then he turned and walked off.

HEY GUYS

"Okay," Elliot said, now that Catalina was here.

He'd been waiting to show us. He swung off his bed and hopped to his chair, which was a pretty cool, high-backed execu-chair from his dad's office, borrowed because it had casters and Elliot could roll around on it. He rolled to his desk.

"These came," he said, poking the keyboard and waiting while the dinosaur screen saver dissipated. "I put them together so we could look at them."

"At what?"

"Just look."

The file that swam up on his screen had three messages.

Dear Bully Lab,

Once this kid started making fun of me because I got a 35 on a spelling test. She called me bacteria brain. On the bus she got these other kids to go "Dumb and Dumber, Dumb and Dumber, Dumb and Dumber." Now she does it all the time.

———

Almost every morning this guy, he's in eighth grade, waits for me. Sometimes he has two people hold my arms so he can hit me. He hits me and hits me. Once he tripped me into a mud puddle, and I had mud on my pants all day in school. He makes me so mad I would like to hurt him really, really bad.

Hey Guys,

It's not so simple as good guys and bad guys, you know. One time I heard this banging in the hallway and I stuck my head out of the room and I saw this big kid throwing this little kid against a locker. He would grab him and throw him again, smash, like it was a game of catch off the wall. Then I started noticing that these two kids are always doing this. Outside at recess the big kid picks up the little kid, twirls him, and smashes him on the ground. You may think this is just cruel bullying and this is what I thought too, at first. But then I noticed the little kid would always scramble right up and say something teasing, like "You can't hurt me, that one didn't hurt"—and then the big kid would chase him and they would do it again. Other kids pick on this little kid, too. He eggs them on. He calls himself the Bouncer. He loves to get pounded. That's true, too.

"I don't get it," I said. "These are from three different kids?"

"Yeah," Elliot said, wiggling on his chair.

"Where'd they come from?"

"They came on KidNet. They were replies to my story. Here's a message that came with one of them . . ."

He worked his mouse and double-tapped.

"Dear Elliot," it said, "here is one story I can tell. Please do the same thing with mine."

"What does he mean, 'the same thing'?" I said.

"He means, send it out. To everyone. Like we did."

I looked at Catalina, who was sitting there wide-eyed.

"So these three kids just read your story," I said, "and they sent you theirs?"

"It's amazing the way you're putting the pieces together," Elliot said.

"Why can't they put their stories out themselves?"

"We're the ones who know how to do that, remember? Besides, this is what we do. Everybody knows that now." He nodded, and crossed his arms.

I said to Catalina, "What do you think?"

She was just shaking her head. "I . . . well. Huh! I guess we should do it. And we should ask people for more."

"Ask for *more*? Why?" I said. "So more kids can get pounded some more?"

"They sent me their stories 'cause they wanted to," Elliot said. "Just like I wanted to send out mine."

I shook my head. "That was crazy, what you wrote. You want to know how much trouble it's already caused? Burke and Blanchette were waiting for me, just a little while ago, so they could tell me they'll kill you if you put out their names."

"Did they say that?"

"That was the general idea."

"Did they hit you or anything?"

"Naw. I'm not scared of those guys."

"Well, neither am I," Elliot said. "So why shouldn't we help other people broadcast what's happened to them? Maybe they won't be so scared anymore either."

I don't know—it bothered me. I was trying to think why.

"You know what it's like?" I finally said. "It's like one of those trashy daytime talk shows. I mean, okay, maybe we could make people famous for five minutes because they're victims. Everybody could read their stories and say, Whoa, their lives are pathetic! And then what? Either these kids get their arms and legs ripped off because they've told on somebody, or a few kids feel sorry for them and everyone else just laughs."

"Geez," Elliot said. "What's the matter with you?"

"Nothing's the matter with me. I just don't think it's a good idea. It'll only make things worse."

"That didn't happen for me," Catalina said softly.

Elliot said, "No?"

"No. It's funny, but ever since we sent out my story, people have been treating me differently. It's like they see me now. Before I was . . . invisible. I didn't mean anything to anybody."

Elliot folded his arms. "Yeah," he said.

I shrugged.

"It's hard to describe exactly," Catalina said. "Bethany stays away from me now. I don't know if she's embarrassed or ashamed or maybe just figuring out what to do next, but so far she hasn't done anything. And the regular kids, even some of the cool kids, they say hi to me now. That's a big difference, you know?"

"And I send my story out and get three stories back," Elliot said. "It's something, Russell. We have to keep doing it."

"But Catalina's story was different," I said. "These kids are just telling about everyday school stuff. Kids who do this stuff *like* to get attention for it."

Elliot sat back and thought. "Okay, how about this?" he said. "We broadcast the messages, but we take off the kids' Net names. No addresses, no authors' names. Then no one knows who they are."

"What if other kids figure out who they are?"

"Russell, these guys *want* us to put their stories out," he said. "They *asked* us to."

"Only one asked."

"They *all* want that," he said. "That's why they sent their stories. Geez." Elliot flopped backward.

But I felt stubborn. "I guarantee you. Putting out stories like this will only make things worse."

"You don't know that," Elliot said.

"I bet you."

"Why don't we find out?" Catalina said.

We both looked at her.

"Well," she said, "we're supposed to be the Bully Lab, right? We're supposed to be experimenting. Why don't we try this and watch what happens? We could put these stories out, anonymously like you say, and ask for more. If we get any more we can put *those* out, and just watch what happens."

Elliot said, "Send these stories to the whole seventh grade, right?"

She shrugged. "Why not all three grades?"

"The *Bully Lab Bulletin*," Elliot mused, sitting up again. "We can send it to every kid in school."

"It's not a good name," I said.

"Why not?" said Elliot.

"It's too . . . young. *Bully Lab* sounds like a little kid thing. It needs to be more powerful." I have to admit, I was getting a little excited about the idea.

"Hmm," Elliot said. "Like what?"

"I don't know. How about . . . *The Justice League*?"

"Name it after a superhero comic? That even sounds nerdy to *me*," Elliot said, grinning now.

"Okay, okay. How about *The Avengers*?"

"TV show," he said. "Really old. They made a movie out of it. Really bad."

"All right, well . . ."

"*The Revealer*," Catalina said.

We looked at her again. "Hey!" Elliot said. "Maybe so."

"Because we're revealing the truth," she said.

"Yeah!" Elliot swiveled to me. "What do you think?"

"It sounds like something on a supermarket rack. *The Revealer*. ALIEN BABIES WITH MULTIPLE HEADS!"

"It does not," Elliot said. "Besides, people *read* those things."

I shrugged. "I guess it's all right with me."

We decided to use Elliot for the contact point, because he was home. This is what we wrote:

The Darkland Revealer

We are three Parkland seventh graders, Russell Trainor, Elliot Gekewicz, and Catalina Aarons. You can reach us at this address on SchoolStream: Troo

We have been the targets of mean cliques and nasty kids, and maybe you have, too. We have definitely seen how bullying and abuse of kids by kids is incredibly common at this school. In fact we think it is probably out of control. The school doesn't do anything about it, so it happens all the time. If you have been affected by it, you know. If you haven't noticed it, it's time you do.

We're not going to tell people why kids do this, because we don't really know. We're not going to tell you some kids are bad and the kids who get picked on are all good, because maybe it's not always that simple.

We just want to tell you true stories. We want to tell people *your* true stories.

We started with two stories of our own. We sent them out on SchoolStream. We didn't expect other kids to send us theirs. But three kids did.

So here are their stories. If you have been affected by evil behavior, send us your story. We will put it in the next *Revealer*. We won't divulge your name.

We are not sure what will happen from this, but we will be interested to find out. Maybe you will be, too—especially after you read about some of the things that go on.

To send us your story, all you have to do is write it in a SchoolStream message, or include it as a file attachment. Just report what happened to you. Tell us the facts.

Sincerely,
The Revealers

We didn't use the word "victim" at all. That was my idea. We added the three kids' stories at the end, with no names or addresses. We pulled down the Distribute menu, and looked at the choices for a minute. Then we chose All.

I thought it was pretty good, what we wrote. I didn't know what was going to happen. But when we got done with the distribution—we just hit the command, and there it went—Elliot spun around, hand up, and I gave him a high five. Then we had to grab him before he fell off his dad's execu-chair.

FOREVER YOURS

We were getting out of social studies the next day when Ms. Hogeboom said, "Oh, Russell."

I stepped out of the funnel of kids cramming for the door.

"I read your *Revealer* on the network," she said.

I blinked. "You did?"

"I did. Is that a problem?"

"Well . . . I thought we only sent it to the kids."

"Well, I got it," she said. "Maybe you sent it to the whole school."

For a second the room rippled. "The *whole school*? Like Mrs. Capelli and everybody?" Mrs. Capelli was the principal. She still is.

"Could be," Ms. Hogeboom said. "I just wanted to say I think it's bold and challenging. It's like an underground newspaper."

"A what?"

She laughed. "Of course you've never heard of an underground newspaper, have you?"

"Uh . . . not really."

"It's a newspaper that challenges the establishment."

Her eyes were sparkling. I had no idea what she was talking about.

"The *establishment* is the way people imagine things have to be," she said. "Especially people who have power."

That word "power" bumped me back to reality. "Like Mrs. Capelli?" I said. My mouth felt dry. You know those fortune-telling eight balls—the ones that you ask a question and shake, and then you look in the window until the answer comes swimming up? I felt as if the answer was swimming up at me, and it was: *You made a big mistake.*

"Well, yes, in part," Ms. Hogeboom said. "But I think the establishment isn't so much people as it is people's *assumptions*. I mean, people assume these sorts of incidents are a fact of life at your age. We tend to say, 'Oh well, kids will be kids.' It's almost like we assume that cruelty and violence are part of growing up. I wonder why we assume that?"

Ms. Hogeboom was pretty much talking to herself at this point. "See how you've made me think?"

"We really didn't mean for grownups to see it," I said.

She nodded. "I wonder what Janet will think," she murmured.

I had a feeling Mrs. Capelli (that's Janet) might not be thrilled. Hadn't we said abuse of kids by kids was out of control at her school? And Mrs. Capelli was a fairly stiff character anyway. She tended to consider your behavior either "appropriate" or "inappropriate"—and there wasn't much doubt in my mind where on that scale this was going to fall.

I suddenly wondered if Mrs. Capelli wasn't the "certain authority figure" that made Mr. Dallas nervous about how we used the Net. "Be careful," he'd said. He probably couldn't bring himself to say, "Be appropriate."

"You better run," Ms. Hogeboom said.

I was thinking the same thing.

Elliot was back that day. After school I was at his locker, holding his crutches while he filled his backpack.

I sagged against the locker. "You know what we did?"

"What?"

"We sent *The Revealer* to the whole school. Not just the kids."

"So what?"

"So *what*? Don't you think that's bad?"

"I don't know. What's wrong with it?"

Just then, Jake Messner stopped by. "Hey, guys," he said.

"Ah . . . hey."

"You know what—it's pretty cool what you're doing," Jake said. "That KidNet thing."

Elliot stared at him.

"Thanks," I said.

"I bet everyone read it—but nobody's saying much," Jake said. He lowered his voice. "What do you think that means?"

"I don't know," I said.

He shook his head. "Me neither. Well, anyway—I hope you keep going with it. Let me know if I can help. Okay?"

"Sure," I said.

He gave a little wave and walked away.

"Don't stand there goggling," I said to Elliot. "You look like a frog."

"Jake Messner said we were cool."

"He didn't say we were cool. He said *The Revealer* kind of was."

"He didn't say *kind of*," Elliot said. "He said pretty cool."

"He's a decent guy."

"And you're worried about people reading the thing," Elliot said. He swung his backpack on and staggered backward on wobbly crutches. I grabbed and steadied him.

"I'm still getting the hang of these," he said. "Hey! That

thing you wrote about Richie punching you. Let's put that in the next *Revealer*."

"What? No way."

Elliot peered at me. "I wrote about the Rots," he said. "Catalina wrote about Bethany."

"Catalina did not write about Bethany."

"Sort of, she did."

"You are not broadcasting what I wrote. I'm serious, Elliot."

"Why? Everybody else is supposed to tell their stories, but you don't need to tell yours?" Elliot started swinging himself down the hall.

"No, I don't need to. And maybe I don't want to."

He stopped. "You're afraid he'll pound you again if you do."

I shook my head. "Actually, I don't think he would. When Burke and Blanchette started threatening me, Richie scared them away. Not that I needed him to," I added quickly.

"So you think he's your buddy now? Richie *Tucker*?"

"No. It's just that he's been acting . . . different. He said I could ask him questions."

Elliot blinked. "Questions?"

"Yeah."

"Well, do! Ask him why he terrorizes people."

"I did that already. He almost broke my face."

"Okay, so ask him *how* he does it. How does he get to people like that? How does he make a person so scared?"

"Hmm," I said. "He might like getting asked that. Or he might break my face."

"I can see it now: PROFILE OF A PREDATOR," Elliot said, holding up one hand like he was scanning a headline. He grinned. "Who wouldn't read *that*?"

When my mom got home she said, "What are you up to tonight?" It was Friday.

I shrugged. "Nothing."

"Well, why don't you see if Elliot and Catalina would like to go to the movies? If it wouldn't be too uncomfortable for him. I think you three ought to do something together."

It wasn't a bad idea. Elliot wasn't sure how his ankle would be if he sat in a chair that long, but he was sick of being home. Catalina hesitated just a second, then she said yes.

The nineplex at the downtown plaza was the place to go. We picked up Elliot first; he hopped into the back and we slid his crutches between the two front seats. They stuck into the back like a divider. When we got to Catalina's, my mom made me go to the door and ring the bell. Catalina came out in tights and a skirt. I'd only seen her in jeans. Suddenly I felt funny about this. I didn't know whether to get back in the front seat or leave it for Catalina. I decided to open the back door and slide in.

My mom turned around quick and gave me a look.

"What?"

"You could open the door for her," she said. "You did it for Elliot."

"Elliot's on crutches."

Catalina got in the front seat. My mom scrunched her face at me in the mirror. Then she smiled at Catalina.

"You look terrific," she said.

"Thank you," Catalina said, and she looked down at her tights. She was quiet. We were all quiet. Suddenly I wanted to be back home on the computer, or watching TV or reading comic books or something. Anything but this.

"What do you three want to see?" my mom asked.

"*Obliterator Three*," I said.

"*Biohazard*," said Elliot.

"I would like to see *Forever Yours*," said Catalina.

My mom scanned us, smiling, with her eyebrows up. "Well, there's something to talk about," she said.

But we didn't. We just sat there.

"Catalina's such a pretty name," my mom finally said.

"Thank you. I was named for the flying boat."

"Pardon?"

"The PBY Catalina. It was an American naval patrol plane in the Pacific during World War II. My grandfather Diodado chose the name. He served with Americans, in the guerrilla campaign. Catalinas flew over to drop supplies."

"Very . . . historic," my mom said.

"Catalina was also a Catholic saint," Catalina said. "And a really big American car."

"A Buick," I said.

"No," my mom said, "a Pontiac. I remember. It was huge."

"That's right. A Pontiac. My grandfather liked all three. But mainly the flying boat."

"Interesting," my mom said.

Catalina shrugged. "That's the Philippines."

Even being in line for the movies was complicated. Halfway up the line in the outer lobby was Bethany and her group. She turned when we came through the glass doors and took in our pitiful little trio, Elliot struggling on his crutches, Catalina hugging herself tight, me looking at anything but my only two friends. A smug smile came over Bethany's face, and she turned regally away. Also partway up the line was Turner White, alone as always, in black as always. Through the glass lobby doors I could see Allison Kukovna and two of *her* friends. The adults and teenagers between all of us were like spacers.

"What are we going to do?" Elliot said.

"About what?"

"Which movie."

"It doesn't matter which movie you say," I said. "You can still go wherever you want inside."

He looked worried, though. Worried and geeky.

"Do they all start at the same time?" he asked.

I looked up at the list. "Yeah," I said. "Pretty much."

When we got to the window, we each said our own movie. When we got inside, Bethany's group had gone ahead, but Allison had held up hers.

"Hi, Catalina," she said. "What are you seeing?" She smiled at us, too. I will give her that. Allison was basically all right.

"I would like to see *Forever Yours*," Catalina said, and glanced back at us.

"Oh, we are, too!" Allison ducked her head. "This is my *third* time. How many times have you seen it?"

"I haven't," Catalina said, huddling into herself.

"Well, my god—come on!"

Allison started to go; then she looked back at us. Her friends looked at each other. Catalina looked at us, too, and we saw what she wanted to do.

"It's okay," Elliot said.

"Yeah," I said. "It's fine."

"Are you sure?" She was almost whispering.

"Definitely."

She turned and was pulled by invisible girl energies into Allison's group. They went off across the lobby, up the carpeted stairs. Elliot and I stood there watching.

"Hey," said a voice behind us, "you don't want to see that goony tearjerker stuff anyway."

It was Turner. He had a big box of licorice. He even ate black candy.

"It's so manipulative," he said. "Impossible true love that can *never be* and then death." He smiled. "For females only."

"We just want death," Elliot said, grinning.

"And car chases," I added.

"There's the manly agenda." Turner offered us licorice. "So, what do two electronic publishers see on their night off?"

I said, "Maybe *Biohazard*."

"Nah," said Elliot, "let's see *Obliterator*."

"*Da Oh-blituratuh*," Turner said. "American filmmaking at its finest. Uh . . . I'll follow you in, all right?"

Turner did follow us in, then he disappeared in the back. Which wasn't hard, for Turner. It seemed like maybe this was his natural element, here in the dark at the movies.

It was best for Elliot to sit midway up, where there was a row with an open space in front of it. A couple of high school guys even got up and moved so he could sit there, and me with him.

At the end of the movie I had that great feeling like I *was* the Obliterator. I swaggered out, but then I had to wait for Elliot, who couldn't swagger very well on his crutches. We didn't see Turner again. In the lobby, Allison and her group came out looking thrilled and clutching each other, like haggard survivors of heartrending love and death. Catalina's face stuck up above the group. It was red, and she wasn't clutching anyone.

My mom was waiting outside in the car. The girls said goodbye to Catalina and moved down the sidewalk, still clinging. We didn't see Bethany again, luckily. She might have gone to *Biohazard*. She'd relate to it.

As we pulled out my mom said, "How was it?"

"Cool!" Elliot said.

I said, "It was pretty intense." But the atmosphere in the car was pretty tense, with Catalina sitting there so straight in the front seat.

My mom said, "Catalina, sweetie, what's wrong?"

Catalina started quivering at first. Then her shoulders were shaking. We could hear soft, melting sort of sounds. Elliot looked at me. I shrugged. My mom reached under the seat and handed Catalina the travel box of Kleenex.

"Was it the movie?" my mom asked.

Her head shook no.

"Did Bethany say something?" Elliot asked, leaning forward. I fought back the impulse to say, "Was it heartrending love and death?"

"What is it, sweetie?" my mom softly urged.

Finally, in a very thin, little-girl voice, Catalina whispered, "I just . . . miss my mom."

My mom held her hand. Oh god, I thought. Why even think about stuff like that? I never let myself think about my dad, not ever. He's just gone.

"Do you talk to her often?" my mom asked.

Catalina shook her head. "My mom can't afford to call, and my dad only lets me once a month."

My mom shook her head. Catalina cried.

"What about e-mail?" Elliot said.

"Not now, Elliot," I whispered.

But my mom turned. Catalina snuffled as her head came up. "Does your mom have a computer?" my mom asked.

"No—my dad brought it with us," Catalina said. "But my cousins have one."

"Is there the Internet in the Philippines?"

"There's the Internet in Borneo," I said.

My mom said, "Russell, please."

"Well, there is. The Internet is everywhere."

"Everybody in Manila uses the Internet," Catalina said. "My mom and I just never needed to, before." She had stopped crying.

"I think you need to now," my mom said.

———

Sometime that night, two kids sent us messages:

These guys make fun of me all the time because most of my friends happen to be girls. They say I'm gay, which I am not. They say I like to wear girl clothes, which I do not. They say I'm really a girl, which I am NOT. I wish I could beat the crap out of them, but I can't.

There's this kid—I'll call him Pugsley (not his real name). He sits behind me in one of my classes, and he just pokes me. He pokes me and pokes me, he does it with a pen in my back so nobody can see. He even does it during tests. I'll be sitting there trying to concentrate and he'll go, poke. Poke. Poke. He also spies over my shoulder at anything I'm doing or looking at. He tries to find out what's important to me so he can trash it.

I liked to wear this hat. (If I told you which hat it is, you'd know who I am.) I couldn't wear it in school, of course, but one time Pugsley saw me drawing a picture of myself with my hat on. That was my mistake (he knew it mattered). Then on Hat Day I made the mistake of bringing (not even wearing) my hat. When we were in class and I got called to the board my backpack was under my desk, open, and he stole my hat. At the end of class it wasn't there. I looked all over for it, my hat! But it was gone. When we got out for recess Pugsley was wearing it.

I said, Give it back. He said, No way, loser! This is my hat! (He was smiling at me.) I said, Give it! I tried to get it but he kept dancing away. I'm pretty small and I couldn't reach it. Then a bunch of kids came and got in a circle, with us in the middle. Pugsley said, You want this hat? You want *this* hat? And he sailed it over my head across the circle. Then another kid picked it up just before I did, and sailed it out of my reach again. Then everybody was doing it and laughing.

Finally the bell rang. Pugsley got the hat one more time and threw it in a mud puddle, and he kicked mucky water on it. Then he stomped on it. I took my hat home and washed it, but it was never really the same hat again. I never took it to school again either. I don't actually wear it much at all anymore.

At dinner on Sunday I mentioned *The Revealer*. My mom wanted to know what I was talking about. So I showed her.

"My god," she said. "They're telling their stories."

"Well, yeah."

"Just like that?" she said. "Just because you gave them the chance?"

"I guess so."

She looked at the computer a while longer. Then she sat back.

"People need to tell their stories," she said. "Don't you think? We don't always get the chance. And here you're giving it to them."

"I guess."

"I think it's wonderful," she said. "Maybe you can tell your story."

"I don't really have a story," I said.

She smiled. "I think you're getting one now."

TROUBLE CENTER

Catalina saw me standing ahead of her in the lunchroom line and started waving, all excited. I waved back and she pointed over to our table in the corner.

When I got there with my tray I found a piece of paper. It was a printout of someone's drawing—a picture, I gradually realized, of us. The three of us. You could see it was us but it was done like a picture from *The Cat in the Hat*. Remember Thing One and Thing Two? That was Elliot and me. They gave us both the silly jumpsuits; Elliot was drawn really scrawny with a big head, and on his chest it said Geek One. I have fairly big ears, I guess, so they made mine flap out from this kid's head with a goofy smile and hair sticking out all over. (Looking at it, I shoved my fingers through my hair.) My jumpsuit said Geek Two. (Hey, not Geek One? No . . . I guess that's Elliot.) The Cat, much taller than us of course, had Catalina's big-eyed face with the squarish bug glasses. Above the drawing in big letters it said: THE CAT & THE RATS.

Catalina came up to the table. Her cheeks were pink and her eyes were bright, but she didn't look upset.

"Listen," she said. "I've got to tell—"

"Oh god, Catalina, this is so incredibly childish!"

That was Allison. She and two of her friends had their trays and were on their way to a more central table. Allison sidled over to stand above Catalina.

"It totally infuriates me," Allison said, glancing up to the ceiling and slumping her shoulders. "Whoever did it e-mailed it to a whole bunch of people. Now they've been printing them and putting them everywhere—you know, wherever the rest of us would see it. I'm *really* sorry." She and her friends had painted their nails with silver-sparkle polish.

Catalina shrugged. "It's kind of clever," she said. She opened her milk and took a sip.

"Well. I wish we knew who did it," Allison said.

"I think we can narrow it down," I said. "Hey, can I have this?" I picked up the paper. "Do you mind?"

Catalina shrugged. "No." She smiled up at Allison patiently, like she was waiting for her to leave.

I folded the paper and put it in my backpack. I was thinking it should at least go into the *Revealer* files, along with those evil girl notes we'd saved.

Allison's friends had already gone to the inner tables. "Well, I better catch up," Allison said, waving as she went.

"Okay," Catalina said. As soon as she was gone, Catalina turned quickly and said, "It's going to work! It is!"

"What?"

"That e-mail idea you had. We had our telephone call last night—I asked my dad if we could have it a week early—and my mom got really excited. She said she'd ask my cousins if she could e-mail me from their computer. Then she called early this morning, before I went to school. They said sure!"

"Hey, that's great."

"She gave me the address, and I sent my first message

right away just to test it. I can't wait till she answers! It's almost like we'll be able to talk every day. Whenever we want. It's *so* great. Thank you!"

"Actually, it was Elliot's idea."

"Well, it's perfect! I don't know why I didn't think of it before."

I shrugged. It was pretty cool, though. I'd never seen her this happy.

"Hey, Catalina, why didn't you want to talk about this with Allison here?"

"I don't know," she said, cutting into her lasagna. "Allison's really nice, and I like her friends. But this is personal."

That afternoon, we had two new messages.

Here are some of the things I have been called: Portly, Pudge, Porkmaster, Beanbag, Tub o' Rama, Gutbucket, Jelly Belly, Super Hippy, Blue Whale, Sumo, Crisco, Pillsbury Doughboy, Doublewide, Thunder Thighs, Blubber Bubble, the Blimp, Supertanker, Butter Butt, Flubber, and the Blob Who Ate Philadelphia. For purebred imbecility, my personal favorite is Oink. They don't actually call me Oink, they just say it when I go by. Isn't that mature?

Believe me, it is not easy to be both physically and mentally larger than most other kids in your grade. They hate you for it. Case in point: Recently I was forced by a certain pent-up need to enter the boys' room, which I would rather never do. Always there is some Cro-Magnon gathering in there. This time two low-life eighth graders, Nate Kroeger and Jason Deep (which he isn't), were admiring themselves in the mirror. I have no idea what they saw to admire.

I tried to get into a stall before they spotted me, but of course, like all hunter-gatherers, they were alert.

"Yo, Blobzilla," said one of the Cave Boys. "Don't eat the toilet paper, okay?" They laughed at that. Imagine.

"At least I won't be contributing to the reading matter on these walls," I said. "Oh, but that's probably above your reading level."

I thought that was fairly good. They pennied me in.

Yes, that's right—they jammed coins in the stall door so that, they thought, I wouldn't be able to get it open. Then they left. I could hear their mindless laughter echoing down the hall.

But don't get any ideas: It didn't work. The edges of the stall door are rounded, as any basic Homo sapiens could notice, so you can't really lodge coins effectively. I pulled hard enough that the door opened, but I fell against the plumbing, bruising my tailbone.

Hey guys: Your brainless prank cost you 38 cents in change. I got all of it, except for two pennies that went into the toilet. I spent it on an extra dessert at lunch.

I'm a boy and these girls follow me home from school, just so they can laugh at me. They walk a ways behind me, and they say, "Going home to your mom, beanpole? Why don't you have any friends, beanpole?" And stuff like that. And they laugh. They whisper things I can't hear, and then they really laugh. My mom said they do it because they secretly like me. That made me feel a little better, for a little while, but I know they don't secretly like me. I wonder why do they do it? Why is it so important to them, to make them do it every day?

"Well, that makes four new stories," Elliot said in the computer lab. "Let's put out a *Revealer*."

"What about this fat kid giving real names?"

"They're not *his* name."

"I don't think we should be giving any names," I said. "They're already calling us rats."

"What're we supposed to do, change what the kid wrote? We can't start doing that. Either we include it or we don't."

"Okay, okay," I said. "Whatever."

This time instead of distributing to All, we selected Grades 6, 7, and 8, one after the other. That way we figured we'd be sending only to kids. *The Revealer* wasn't for Mrs. Capelli and the teachers—and we weren't rats, in my opinion, if we were only telling kids.

When we were finishing, Mr. Dallas came over. He was pretty excited, even for him. "Hey, guys! I saw your e-publishing thing," he said. "Are you going to do another one?"

"We just did," I said.

Mr. Dallas nodded, but then he shook his head, like he was having an argument with himself. "You know, I love what you're doing," he said. "It's an inspired use. But . . . it's also got you guys in the scope."

"In the what?"

His lips pressed tight. "People are aware of this. I don't mean just the students. You also sent this thing to the powers that be."

"That was a mistake," I said. "We're not doing that again."

He nodded. "That's good—but you're already in the scope. I mean, it's not that you're doing anything wrong. Just try not to . . ."

We waited. "Not to what?"

"I don't really know," he said, and he smiled and shrugged. "I guess I'm just nervous. Giving students open access to a schoolwide LAN is an experiment—it's only a one-year trial, and I really had to argue, plead, and wheedle to get *that* approved. The powers that be are pretty uneasy about it. What you're doing helps prove how much kids can do with this. I just . . . well, I guess I just hope it doesn't get us into something we can't control."

"But something is happening," Elliot said. "We're not really controlling it."

"Yes," he said. "Yes! I can see that. I see kids all over school, reading your thing. You've put the network on the edge. That's where it should be. We'll just see what happens. Hey! Listen, something else. I'm organizing something new for next month. We're calling it the Creative Science Fair. To enter, you have to develop something that has experimental or other scientific value, something that wasn't there before you started. Something you create. Get it?"

"Uh, sure," Elliot said.

"Think it'll catch on?"

Elliot looked at me. "I don't know," I said. "Maybe."

"Well, anyway," Mr. Dallas said, "you three make a good team. You might think about doing something."

"Okay," I said. "We'll talk about it." But I figured we probably had enough to work on.

"All right," he said with gusto. "Great!"

We were out in the hall, hurrying, almost late for last block, when Burke came the other way. Elliot was flinging his crutches ahead and swinging through on them—he was getting pretty good at that. Burke, passing, flicked his foot to stop one of the crutch tips so the other crutch came down ahead of Elliot but the blocked one didn't and Elliot tilted, flailing at a bad angle, and clattered to the floor. I tried to catch him but I couldn't. He was down and his crutches were spread out wide like wings. When I looked up, Burke was gone.

"Aw, *man*," Elliot said. He rolled over slowly, pulling his hands loose. "He did that on purpose, didn't he?"

"Yeah."

He shouted, *"You're an ass, Burke!"*

I winced. It echoed down the hall, nearly empty now, with almost everyone in class.

Quick *tap-tap-tapping* footsteps started coming our way. Elliot was just back on his feet when the principal came around the corner.

"Mr. Gekewicz. Could that *possibly* have been you I just heard?"

Elliot nodded.

"He had his crutch kicked out from under him," I said.

Mrs. Capelli didn't look at me. "That kind of language is a level-two infraction, Mr. Gekewicz. It's totally inappropriate, and I will *not* have it in my school. Automatic detention this afternoon. Room 202." She spun on her heel to leave.

"Hey, wait," I said. "You mean it's okay to kick a kid's crutches out from under him, but it's not okay to get mad about it?"

She turned back and peered at me. "We base disciplinary measures on infractions we have visually seen, or for which we have reliable evidence, Mr. Trainor. And we definitely *do* insist on appropriate verbal expression. Which does not include swearing in the halls."

Mrs. Capelli was short, with short blond hair, and she always stood very straight as if she was trying to be taller. She had bulging eyes, with heavy eyelids like curtains lowered halfway. Peering at you that way, she always looked like she didn't believe you. Which, generally, she didn't.

"Well," I said to Elliot, "I guess visually seeing is believing."

He grinned. Mrs. Capelli's breath sucked in like an angry hiccup. "Suddenly you two are becoming a trouble center," she said. "I have no idea what's come over you, but if this is what you want, this is what you'll get. Room 202. Immediately after school. Both of you.

"You'll be able to think about whether you want to spend a *lot* more time there," Mrs. Capelli added as she tap-tapped away.

In detention, Elliot passed me a note.
I can't believe you talked back to the principal, he wrote.
I wrote back, *I didn't. I was talking to you.*
Right.
Anyway, that's so stupid. Visually seeing.
Elliot quickly scribbled back. *THIS is the kind of thinking that creates a Trouble Center!*
I gave him a thumbs-up. The teacher looked our way, and we both studiously scrutinized our scrap-torn notebook pages.

We split up outside. I cut across the parking lot and walked to Convenience Farms. It was high time for a root beer.

While I was in there closing the cooler door and holding my bottle, Richie came in. He went to the counter.

I went up and put the plastic bottle on the counter, beside his pack of Winstons. We both paid. He turned and pushed open the door with his back, looking at me and lifting his eyebrows. I put the root beer in my backpack and zipped it up quick.

Outside, Richie was zipping open his cigarettes.

"So," he said. "Let me ask you something."

I waited. He looked out at the street. Put a cigarette in his mouth.

"I hear you're publicizing the bad guys in school," he said, lighting up. "That's what I hear."

"Yeah, kind of," I said. "Like you said, remember? Put the squids in their place?"

Richie took a drag. "What are you doing, exactly?" he said, letting the smoke come out and drift away.

"Well, we're putting kids' stories on SchoolStream."

"On what?"

"You know. KidNet."

"Oh. Yeah. What kind of stories?"

"Well, mainly about kids getting picked on. And stuff."

"*And stuff,*" he said. He flicked his cigarette. "So," he said. "What about me?"

"Huh?"

"Huh? *Huh*? What are you, stupid? What'd you say about me?"

I shrugged. "Nothing."

"That's what I heard," he said. "*Nothing.* So what do you think you're doing?"

"What?"

He cocked his head. "*Huuh? Whuut?* Listen, kid, I know you're not retarded, but I'll try to say this nice and slowly. You start telling the whole school about the bad kids—ooh, the *mean* kids—and you don't say anything about me? *Nothing?*"

I blinked. "You *want* us to say something about you?"

He shrugged, smiling a little. "Well, hey. Who's the most feared person in this school?"

"I guess you?"

"You guess. You *guess.* You were scared half to death."

"Well . . ."

"Of course you were. So why don't you put that on your KidNet?" He took a drag, crossed his arms, and waited.

I remembered what Elliot had said. I wondered.

"You said I could ask you questions."

"Yeah."

"So what if I did?"

"What if you did what?"

"Well, I could ask you questions—like, how do you get kids to be so scared? I mean, really. How do you do it?"

Richie nodded, with a half smile. "Not a bad question."

"And what you say, I mean your answers, I could put them on the Net. Like a profile. You *are* good at that stuff."

"The *best*."

"Sure. So will you do it?"

He shrugged. "Okay. But no questions I don't like."

"No questions you don't *like*? What questions won't you like?"

Richie smiled. "Maybe you'll find out."

"Oh. Great."

"Tomorrow," he said. He dropped his cigarette and ground his boot heel on it. "Activities block. In the boiler room."

"The boiler room?"

He started walking. He was past the gas pumps.

"Be there," he said, without looking back.

"O . . . kay," I whispered to myself. I watched him go. I unzipped the backpack, reaching for my root beer.

My hands were shaking.

When my mom got home she said, "How was your day?"

"Pretty interesting."

That night I got a message from Elliot:

> Did you read in the paper that they've found a little dinosaur fossil with feathers? It's so cool! They found it in China. It's like a small fast dinosaur only it has feathers all over its body. It finally proves that small fast dinos evolved into birds.
>
> I think we should have a slogan on *The Revealer*:
> EVOLUTION HAPPENS

Well, I wasn't sure what that had to do with anything. But Elliot had his own way of seeing things.

SICKOLOGISTS

Catalina got an e-mail answer from her mom. She called that night to tell me. She was really happy. I asked her about the Cat and the Rats thing. She said she didn't care.

I said, "She's trying to put us in our place."

"Who is?"

"Bethany. Don't you think she was behind it?"

"Oh, I guess so. Probably."

"Sure. She wants people to see us as rats, or losers, so they won't pay us any more attention. I bet she hates that we're getting attention in the first place."

"But does it really matter that much? I mean, next week people will be talking about something else."

"Bethany'll still hate you, though."

For a second, Catalina didn't answer.

"I used to think it meant something bad about me, that she acts that way," she said. "Now I think a person like that just needs someone to plot against. She needs enemies. But really, so what? The whole world is not Parkland School."

"Some people think it is."

"Well, it isn't."

"Yeah." And then I told her about Richie—about the boiler room.

"He says I can't ask him any questions he doesn't like."

"What questions doesn't he like?"

"I don't know! What should I do?"

She chuckled. "Well, I don't know. Ask about his home life. Ask about his friends."

"I'm pretty sure Richie Tucker has no friends."

"Well, what do you want to know about him?"

"I just want to know what's *with* him. How come he terrorizes people in the first place? I mean, why do that?"

Another pause.

"That might not be the best way to start," Catalina said.

"I know. I'm dead."

"No, don't think that way. My dad works in sales and marketing. He says you can talk to anybody—you just have to find something you have in common."

"Something in common? Me and Richie?"

"Yes. Why not? There must be something."

"We have him beating me up in common."

"Well, there you go!" She started laughing, then she stopped. "But really. There must be something. I mean, more than that."

"I don't know. Maybe I'll find out. If I live."

We had a project due for social studies that day, the rough draft of a personal essay on the subject "What I Think Anne Frank Was Really Like As a Person." In class Ms. Hogeboom paired us up to conference on the drafts. Bethany DeMere got me.

She was outraged. After we pulled our desks together—actually, I pulled mine over to hers—she scraped her desk around so that it was angled away from me. Then, as she sat there, she caught the glance of one of her friends and rolled her eyes at the ceiling, and shook her hair. Her mouth was shut tight.

I liked that. Two weeks ago Bethany did not even know I existed. I guess she did now.

While I read her rough draft she gazed at the ceiling, sighed, and tapped her fingernails on her desk.

I'm very sorry but I do think Anne Frank was actually a fairly annoying person. I mean, she thought she was so much smarter than everyone else in that Annex, and she thought she was so attractive to all the boys when she was still in the school, even though in the pictures she has plain dark hair and looks very ordinary, if you ask me. But the main thing is she thought she was above everyone else.

She was writing about how cruel the Nazis were, which everyone knows they were, but she also kept writing how nasty and small-minded everyone was who was stuck living with Anne, too. I mean, I think the Nazis were terrible just like everyone else. But why does that have to make Anne Frank so wonderful? Just because she wrote all about herself and how sensitive *she was. I do not think Anne Frank had the most attractive personality. Maybe you think I am terrible for thinking that. But I kind of do.*

I took a deep breath. It wasn't every day that a person got to comment on the deep personal thoughts of Bethany DeMere. My heart was thumping a little, but I was also psyched.

"Well . . . it's interesting," I said.

Bethany sighed. Without looking at me she held out her hand, palm up, like: *Give it back, you paramecium.*

But not yet.

"How come you say the most annoying thing about Anne was how she . . . let me see . . . 'She thought she was above everyone else'? I mean, Bethany, nobody acts that way more than you do."

"*Excuse* me?"

"Oh, come on. Everybody knows it. You have to be number one, and if anybody threatens that, you make them pay."

She looked away.

I said, "You know who I'm talking about."

She glanced at me quickly. I smiled. She crossed her arms and stared at the ceiling. "We're supposed to be conferencing," she said. "I don't have to talk about anything else besides that."

"Okay. If you'd been in that attic with Anne, and that boy was paying more attention to her than you, what would you have done to her?"

Bethany's face flared. "*Ms. Hogeboom,*" she said.

"Bethany? Russell? Are you conferencing?"

"Yes," I said.

"*No,*" said Bethany.

"Well . . . keep trying."

Bethany snorted. "It's not fair," she said to me fiercely. "You're a nobody who suddenly thinks you're somebody. You and your friends. But that doesn't give you the right to say nasty things about me or anybody else."

She actually looked hurt.

"Huh," I said. "So what gives you that right?"

She shook her head. "If you're not going to talk about my draft, I don't care what happens. I'm not talking to you."

"All right." I was reading the paper again. "Here, you say how Anne 'wrote all about herself and how sensitive she was.' "

Bethany looked at me uncertainly. "So?"

"So do you think it's so wrong if somebody writes the

truth about who they really are? Do you think it's so bad when other people read it?"

Bethany flushed a deep red. She grabbed her notebook, opened it, and scribbled furiously. She ripped out the page and slapped it on my desk.

I'm not talking to you ANYMORE, the paper said. *I don't care WHAT* happens.

"Okay," I said. I folded the paper and put it in my pocket. Then I leaned over and whispered, "But this isn't over."

She glared at me. *"You bet it's not,"* she replied.

In the lunchroom line Elliot was picking up his tray with one hand while he leaned on both crutches held together. I caught up to him at the cash register.

"Hey," I said, "I'll take the tray."

"No. Not today."

"Why not?"

"Here," he said, handing me one crutch. "Just take this."

"Why?"

But he just leaned over and picked at his milk carton till it was open on top. Then he took off, poling himself across the floor toward the tables, holding his tray by one edge. I followed.

Among the center tables, Elliot came up to where Burke and Blanchette were sitting side by side. Blanchette glanced up and opened his big, half-mocking smile just as Elliot suddenly stumbled and his tray launched forward, tipping as the milk sloshed out. Everything landed and splashed all over Burke.

Blanchette grinned even wider. "Why, *Geek*owitz!" he said.

Burke stood up. He had milk, spaghetti, and butterscotch pudding all over his shirt and his pants. His face was turning very, very red.

"You slimy disgusting little jerkoff—I swear you'll pay for this."

"Hey, man, it was an accident," Elliot said. "See, I'm hurt. I have to use these crutches. I have a lot of accidents."

He turned and poled back expertly toward me. He had a bright look of pure delight. I handed him his crutch.

"Excellent menu today," he said.

"They're going to kill you."

He shrugged. "They already tried that."

The Darkland Revealer

The kid who's after me has spit in my food in the lunchroom, stuffed me in a garbage can in the bathroom, stolin my clothes in the locker room, whipped iceballs at me on the playground, and thrown my backpack out the window of the bus. I don't want to come to this school anymore. Every day I don't want to come. I get stomickaches and headaches. But I have to come anyway.

The worst part is the kid always gets out of it. When he gets caught he's such a good lier. The other day he was going to the shower in the locker room to throw my clothes in there and the jim teacher stopped him. He said he thought they were his clothes and he was only looking for a place to change with privissy, because the other kids were picking on him. He actually almost started to cry. The jim teacher believed him. The teachers always believe him. I know he will always get out of trouble, and he knows it too. So he knows he can do anything. And so do I.

There was this girl last year who just did everything wrong. I mean she wore really wrong clothes, like Disney sweatshirts that were dirty anyway and patent leather shoes, and she said really ridiculous things trying to fit in. She just was awkward in everything, like some kids are if you know what I mean. So right away a certain group of girls especially started harassing her.

On the playground when this girl would come out this group would make sure nobody did anything with her, so she would sit there by herself. Then that got boring for them so they started saying things, like that the girl lived in a trailer (I don't know if that was true) and she had cat hair all over her clothes and she was stupid. Then other kids would join in making fun of this girl. I joined in too.

One time there was a whole group of us making fun of her and saying she dressed like a Salvation Army reject and she slept with her cats and stuff like that (and I was doing it too) when the girl picked up a rock and threw it. She hit one of the leaders of the group that had started it in the head, and she was bleeding all over the place. Everybody ran away. The girl who threw the rock was crying and so was the girl she hit, who went running into the school. She had to have stitches and the girl who threw the rock was suspended for three days and had to see a counselor. So as soon as she came back to the playground ALL the girls surrounded her and said she belonged in a cave and she was crazy and had to see a sickologist. I was in that group again. I felt really bad because I knew what really happened. But I didn't say anything about it and I didn't stop.

You should say more about what girls do. They can really be more vicious. I should know. I am a girl, and this is what I did to someone.

Last year when I was in seventh grade, this girl was new and I didn't like her, I didn't want her to be popular. At first I just told people she had no friends and was weird. But I knew she would start to get friends eventually. So I became the girl's friend myself. I acted really friendly with her. I told her people wanted to be friends with her, and she should have a party at her house and everyone would come. She got excited and we worked on the invitations together. She sent them out to a bunch of girls. Then I went to all the girls and said we were playing a joke, and not to come to the party. So on the day of the party, I know the girl was really excited and she had rented movies and she had all this food and stuff because she told me she was going to. And absolutely nobody showed up. Not one person. Including me.

That girl never came back to our school. She went to a private school I heard. I know I did a terrible thing, but at the time I didn't care. Now I do care. I wish I had not done it. I do feel terrible about it. I read these stories and think about it.

So I just want people to know that girls can be the worst. But we should think about what we do sometimes.

THE BOILER ROOM

I wondered how I could get down what Richie would say, so I'd have his actual words. I didn't want to take notes. I finally decided that, if he would let me, I would use a tape recorder.

My mom had one. It was an old portable cassette recorder. I told her I needed to borrow it for a school project, which was pretty much true. (It was a project, and it was going to happen in school.) I went to the drugstore that night and bought new batteries and a sixty-minute tape.

"A tape recorder?" Elliot said the next morning, crutching up the school steps beside me. The thing was hanging by its handle from my hand.

"Yeah. I want to get what he really says. You know?"

"Hmm," Elliot said. "So. Are you nervous?"

"Yeah." I felt a shiver.

"What are you going to ask him?"

"I have no idea."

He stopped and looked at me. "You have a tape recorder but no questions?"

"Okay, shut up now. Okay? You're not helping."

He shrugged. "All right. Where are you going to meet him?"

"In the boiler room."

"The *boiler* room?"

"Oh, that's reassuring."

"Are people allowed in there? I've never been down there. Have you?"

"No. But this is Richie."

Elliot nodded. "Well, I think it'll be great if you get something for *The Revealer*. Something really different. Maybe . . . INSIDE THE MIND OF A PREDATOR."

"Yeah. Maybe."

"Or how about: RUSSELL TRAINOR'S LAST WORDS. Hey, good thing you'll have it on tape!"

"Elliot."

"I could add a personal tribute. 'He was my friend. He was brave. He wasn't bright, but he was brave.' "

"Elliot, will you shut up?"

He stopped short, hopping a little on his crutches. "I'm sorry, man. I was just joking."

"You're really bad at it."

"Yeah." He thought a second. "You know, actually, it's almost like you're a detective. An investigator. It's what we wanted to do: solve a mystery."

"Yeah."

"Of course, most mysteries involve murders."

"*Elliot* . . ."

Mrs. Capelli was standing outside the main office.

"Mr. Gekewicz," she said, stepping forward as we came up.

"Hi, Mrs. Capelli."

The principal folded her arms. "I understand you dumped your lunch on a classmate yesterday."

"That's true, I did. It was an accident."

"Yes, I'm sure it was. But, interestingly, I'm told by a faculty member who witnessed the incident that you seemed somehow pleased by it."

She peered at him from beneath those heavy eyelids.

"Mr. Gekewicz, is there any possibility that the student who received your accidental dumping might have been the one who you say kicked your crutches on Monday?"

Elliot shrugged. "That would be an incredible coincidence."

Her eyes narrowed. "It would, wouldn't it?"

I couldn't help myself. "But, Mrs. Capelli," I said, "you didn't believe us when we told you that happened. How come you believe it now?"

She shot me a look. "Mr. Trainor. Did you enjoy detention on Monday?"

"Well, actually, you know, it felt kind of safe."

Her head drew back. She looked puzzled. Then she seemed to be thinking. "Have you two sent out another of your . . . story collections?"

"Well, yes," Elliot said. "Yes, we have."

"You have? Then why haven't I seen it?"

"Well, we really only did it for kids."

She didn't look happy. "I'm not sure I'm comfortable with that," she said. "I'm not sure I'm comfortable with this whole thing. You two used to be so quiet. Now suddenly . . ."

She shook her head. "There's no reason to be reckless," she said.

"We're not trying to be reckless, Mrs. Capelli," I said.

"I just would like to know what's going on." She turned and tap-tapped back into her office.

We had finally made it to Elliot's locker when Leah Sternberg came up. She's that helpful kid who's on Student Council and everything else.

"I want to tell you guys I think it's great what you're doing," she said.

"It is?"

"Oh, definitely."

Elliot said, "Why?"

Leah's forehead crinkled. "Well, lots of kids didn't know these things were going on. Myself included. I think this is going to make a big difference."

"Really?" Elliot said. "How?"

She crossed her arms, like Mrs. Capelli. "Well, this is our school. If people can't do rotten things in secret anymore, they probably won't do them."

"But a lot of people don't do things in secret," I said. "They do them right in front of everyone."

"But you're changing the atmosphere. I mean, middle school kids won't do things if they're not cool to do. Right?"

"Well, that's true," Elliot said.

"That's why you've got to keep on doing this."

"Okay," I said, impressed. "Thanks."

Elliot watched Leah bustle off. "Wow," he said. "Maybe this *is* doing something. People are definitely treating us different."

"Yeah. It's kind of strange."

"What's strange?" said Catalina, coming up. She had a computer disk in her hand.

Elliot said, "Feeling like somebody."

"Everybody is somebody," she said.

"Not usually," I said. "How's your mom?"

"She's good." Catalina smiled a big smile. "I had three messages from her last night. Nothing special, just telling me about her day. Hey, somebody stuck this on my locker." She held out the disk.

"Who?" Elliot said.

"I don't know. It was Scotch-taped on there."

"It's probably another story," I said. "We can put it in the next issue."

"We should meet," Elliot said. "I might have more stories in my e-mail."

"I can't meet at activities," I said. "How about after school?"

"In the computer lab?"

"Okay."

"I won't have much time," Catalina said. "I have to practice." She held up her saxophone case.

Elliot winced. "Don't worry," he said. "We'll get out of there fast."

She swung the case at him. He dodged expertly on his crutches.

Activities block.

The boiler room.

Oh, man.

I had signed into computer lab, then snuck out, down the basement hall. I slowly opened the heavy louvered door, just enough to stick my head in. It was chilly in the hall, but now the warmth of the boiler room floated up to my face. It *smelled* hot. From deep inside came the furnace's low throbbing sound. I took a breath and slipped in.

I was standing on a railed metal platform. Below me in the dim room sat the furnace, a big green metal box. Fat, squarish white pipes ran up from the furnace and filled the whole ceiling. No doubt covered with asbestos. I thought, I'll probably get cancer . . . if I live that long.

The gray cinder-block walls had whitish stains and dark seepage running down them. A beat-up wooden desk sat facing the wall, covered with cardboard boxes of nuts and bolts. By the desk was an old wooden chair; on the wall was a calendar with a waxy color picture of a girl with a very big build, in a red bikini, holding a giant red monkey wrench. Whoa!

The door behind me squeaked open. Richie stepped in.

He shut the door and ignored me as he walked down the spiral metal staircase. He pulled out the old chair and sat down. He glanced up at me and raised his eyebrows.

When I started to circle down the steps, he spotted the thing hanging from my hand.

"What the hell is that?"

"It's a tape recorder."

"I know what it is. What the hell is it for?"

I started shaking. But I told myself: Okay. Walk down the stairs. You're in this. Go.

I went. When I got to the desk, I laid the recorder on it. "See . . . this way I figured I could get what you really say. I wouldn't get your words wrong. See?"

He shrugged. "Okay. I guess. But if I don't like something I'm turning it off."

"If you don't like something you can erase it."

"Riiight."

I stood there, without a chair. Richie nodded over to a pile that filled the murky space behind the spiral stairs, under the metal platform: old classroom chairs and desks tossed in a jumble. On a chair up front was taped a sign on lined paper: BROKEN CHAIR—DO NOT SIT.

I pulled out a different chair, brought it over, and sat down near the edge of the desk, so I could reach the tape-recorder buttons but be as far away from Richie as possible.

I held my fingers over the Play and Record buttons, which you had to hit together if you wanted to record. I said, "All right?" Richie shrugged. I pressed the buttons, and the tape started turning.

I still did not know what to ask. He was gazing up at the calendar.

"How come we can be in here?" I finally blurted out.

He snorted. "What the hell kind of question is that?"

"I don't know, I didn't think kids were . . ."

"What, you think I don't have friends? You think I don't know anybody?"

"No. I mean, I don't know."

"Look, are you gonna ask stupid questions? 'Cause I don't have time for stupid questions."

"Okay. You said to me, 'Fair is fair.' Right?"

"Yeah . . ."

"So how come you pick on younger kids? Smaller kids?"

He shrugged. "That's the way the world is, kid. You don't like it . . ." He folded his fist up slowly. "I can give you a ticket out."

"For god's sake, Richie. Why do you *say* stuff like that?"

He smiled. "Stuff like what?"

"I don't know. Like you're the dad from hell or something."

His smile vanished. "You take that back," he said in a higher voice. He stood partway up.

"You take that *back*!"

"Uh . . ."

He was in my face. *"You take it BACK!"*

"Okay, Richie. Okay. I'm sorry."

"It's not *TRUE*."

"Okay. I believe you."

Richie looked around jerkily. Then he settled down. He sat. He looked away from me, and didn't say anything.

I was trying to think. I remembered what Catalina said, about finding something in common. So I said, "I don't have a dad. He died when I was a baby. I guess I don't know . . ."

"You can kiss my ass."

"What?"

"You can kiss my ass, all right? I don't give a shit what you have and don't have. This isn't supposed to be"—he put on that whimpering, mocking face—"about *yooou*."

"You know, you're really full of it," I said.

"What?"

I don't know what got into me, but I said, "You figure you can go pushing people around and that makes you so great. Is that all you can do, act like a tough guy? Is that *it*?"

"That's another stupid question."

"Okay, why? I really want to know. Why?"

He got right in my face. "You're on thin ice right now, mister, you know that? *Really* thin ice. I'm telling you: Push me one more inch and, so help me, I'll teach you a lesson you will *never* forget."

"You do talk like a dad from hell!" I blurted out. "Is *that* it?"

Total silence.

Oh my god.

Then he exploded.

"You *shut up*! You *shut your damn face*, all right? You *SHUT UP*!" He stood over me, shaking, and his face was very weird. His punching hand drew back in a fist, then un-fisted, then clenched again.

Richie's eyes darted around and landed on the tape recorder. He lunged and grabbed its handle, lifted the little machine up and held it with both hands. His face was silent and wild.

"Don't," I breathed. "Please don't. It's my mom's."

He swung back and smashed the thing against the end of a spiral staircase. With a *thunk* the machine shattered and bits of it flew everywhere—chunks hit the back wall and scraps clattered into the pile of chairs.

Richie stood there, looking into that darkness. From the handle in his hand hung little wires and wreckage.

He dropped the thing. It hit the floor, and without looking back he climbed up the spiral staircase.

"I'm sorry, Richie," I said. "I'm sorry."

At the top, Richie turned and looked at me, and for just a second he looked incredibly sad. Then he tightened his mouth and shook his head, hard.

"I told you no stupid questions," he said in his tough-guy voice.

"I'm sorry." I didn't mean about the questions.

He looked down at me.

"You can't tell anybody about this," he said.

"I know."

"Not ever. You can't."

"I won't. I wouldn't."

He looked down at the floor. Then he sucked himself up straight. "Pick up that mess—or there'll be trouble," he said. "I'm warning you."

He turned, opened the door, and was gone.

"I don't have a story," I told Elliot in the computer lab.

"Why not?"

I shrugged. "He didn't say much."

"Nothing on tape?"

I shook my head. "The tape recorder doesn't work."

"Oh. You didn't test it?"

"Yeah. It worked before."

"Oh. It's old, huh?"

"Yeah. Kind of beat-up."

"Huh." He seemed distracted, like he was also thinking about something else.

"Here's something," Catalina said, sitting at a computer.

I'm scared to write this story but I want to tell the truth. I don't like what I'm being made to do. It's not right. Please help me tell this story.

I'm a seventh-grade girl, and I wanted to be in the most popular group. That meant I had to be accepted by Bethany DeMere.

"What's this?" Elliot said.

Everybody in the seventh grade knows Bethany D. Anybody would say she is the most popular and powerful girl in our grade. If you want to be in her group, that means you have to be accepted by her. I wanted that so much, I said I would do what she told me I had to do.

It's so hard for me to write this—I feel so ashamed of myself. Maybe if you would put this in your *Revealer* so the truth would come out I would feel better. I hope so.

Bethany said if I wanted to be in her group I would have to write her paper. For social studies. I didn't want to do it but I said I would. I felt sick the whole time, but I did it. I wrote a paper for her about Anne Frank. I wrote that Anne Frank was actually a fairly annoying person, and did not have the most attractive personality. I felt TERRIBLE writing this, because Anne Frank is my hero! But Bethany said that's what I had to say.

Maybe you will say it was worth it, because her group is the coolest group in the grade. But I am feeling sick about what I did. I'm not brave enough to tell this myself. I hope you will please put this in your *Revealer*, and tell people the truth.

"Wow!" Elliot said.
I was staring at the screen.

"It's true," I said.

"It is?"

"Yeah. I read that essay. We got paired up to conference, remember? I read it. That's exactly what it said."

Catalina was still looking at it.

"I don't know," she said. "It gives Bethany's name."

"So?" I said. "We already did that."

"We did?"

"Yeah. With that story about the kid in the toilet. Remember? He gave names, and nobody said anything about it."

"But . . . I don't know," she said. "This gives me a funny feeling."

"Catalina, this is your personal tormentor," Elliot said.

"I would almost feel bad for her, though, if this came out. I mean, that's cheating."

"Yeah, and she *did* it," I said. "Look, we will never get a better chance to take Bethany down. And *nobody* deserves to get taken down more than Bethany!" I was still feeling rattled. But this I didn't have to think about.

"We could take the name out," Catalina said. "Everyone would still know it's her."

"But this girl wrote it this way. She *wants* us to tell the truth." I pointed to the message. "See? That's what she says. Anyway, I don't think we should start changing what people write. We talked about that before. Either we send it as is or we don't."

Catalina shrugged.

"All right," she said. "Should we wait for more stories?"

"What the heck," Elliot said. "Let's get it out there."

She nodded. Across the top, she typed *The Revealer*.

"Let's leave out 'Darkland' from now on," she said. "It's a bit much."

"Sure," I said. "Whatever."

"Show me how to do this again. You pull down Send . . ."

Elliot leaned over. "Distribute. That's it. Hold the shift down. Now select Grade 6 . . . 7 . . . 8. That's it. Now hit Send."

Catalina sat back. The little Sending window came on the screen, and then it was gone.

"Amazing that you saw that one essay, so you knew to believe this," Elliot said to me as we left the lab.

"Yeah," I said. "Tough break, princess."

THE OFFICE

✳Two mornings later we got pulled out of homeroom. All three of us. A note came instructing us to report to Mrs. Capelli's office.

In the hall, Catalina was bug-eyed and silent. Elliot whispered, "What is it?" I shook my head. I thought maybe it was about being in the boiler room. But no. That would be just me.

We went slowly down the hall. From the classrooms came ordinary murmuring. I wished I was in there, in an ordinary class.

In the office, the secretary behind the counter flicked her head toward Mrs. Capelli's closed door. It said PRINCIPAL on the frosted glass.

"They're waiting for you," she said.

Elliot mouthed, *"They?"* Catalina nudged me forward.

I turned the knob and the door clicked open. Inside, Mrs. Capelli sat rigid behind her desk. Mr. Dallas, red-faced, fidgeted in a chair. And there was a man in a suit.

The man was sitting in a chair, holding a briefcase on his

lap. He had pale hair and a pale mustache. I knew I'd seen him before; then I remembered. He was Bethany's dad.

I stood in the doorway. Catalina and Elliot bumped up behind me.

"You're in the right place, Mr. Trainor," Mrs. Capelli said. She nodded toward three empty folding chairs, set up side by side.

We sat.

"You know Mr. Dallas," she said. He nodded quickly at us. With no gusto.

"And this is Mr. DeMere. His daughter, Bethany DeMere, as I believe you know, is your classmate."

Bethany's dad nodded in our general direction.

"Mr. DeMere is an attorney."

"Yes?" said Elliot.

"Yes," Mrs. Capelli said. "A lawyer."

Mr. DeMere was looking past us, as if we weren't worth seeing. Just like the lovely Bethany.

Mrs. Capelli folded her hands and leaned forward. "Would you care to tell us why you think Mr. DeMere might be here?"

We just looked at her.

"All right, perhaps Mr. DeMere will explain. Mr. De-Mere?"

The guy clicked open his briefcase. He pulled out a paper. He held it by the top two corners with his thumbs and fore-fingers only, like it was odious. He turned toward us and held it out. I saw that it said *The Revealer*. A hot flush fell down my face and chest and arms.

"Two days ago," Mr. DeMere said, "did you three e-mail this . . . anecdote about my daughter to the entire student body of this school?"

Mrs. Capelli glared at Elliot. He nodded.

"What was the source of this anecdote?" Mr. DeMere said.

"We don't know," I said.

"You don't know."

"Well, no. It was anonymous."

"How did you get it?"

"Someone left it at Catalina's locker."

"Did you write it?" he said to me.

"*No.* I told you. It was on a computer disk taped to her locker door."

"Do you know who wrote it?"

"No. It was anonymous."

"Do you know that it's false? Do you know that it's a piece of libelous fiction?"

He looked at us, one after another. Catalina sat there like a wax statue of herself.

"One of her friends wrote it," Elliot said quickly. "She didn't want to use her name 'cause she'd be out of the group."

"How do you know that?"

"Well . . . that's what she wrote."

"That's what she wrote," Mr. DeMere said slowly. "Of course, *any*one can write *any*thing. Couldn't they?"

When we didn't answer, he took a breath. "This is a pretty wild story—saying there's some kind of girls' mafia here. Did you just assume it was true? Did any of you do anything to find out?"

We didn't answer.

Mr. DeMere cleared his throat. "So without checking anything you broadcast to the entire school a story that accuses my daughter, an honor-roll student since the fourth grade, of systematic cheating. Do you have *any* idea how serious an allegation that is?"

He looked right at us. "If in fact this were true, she could be suspended—or worse," he said. "This would go on her permanent transcript." He shook his head. "Do you know how seriously something like this could affect her life?"

I could hear a clock ticking.

"How do you know it's not true?" said Elliot.

"I'll tell you how. First, I have questioned every one of her close friends. Every single one of them knows nothing of this. Second, I have questioned my daughter, whom I trust. Third, my daughter does her homework at the kitchen table. Either my wife or I have watched our daughter work on every single one of her essays for social studies this year. We look at her work. Every night. We looked at this essay the night our daughter wrote it. In her own handwriting."

He stared straight at me. "So every single person who might know anything about this story you've shared with the whole school has said, and will testify if necessary, that it is false. It's fiction. It has no basis *whatsoever*."

He slapped the paper back down in his briefcase and clicked the locks shut. He looked at Mrs. Capelli, crossed his arms, and just sat there.

The principal shook her head. She spoke more softly than I expected. "Didn't it occur to you three that if you were given an anonymous story, someone might have made it up? Don't you think you might have looked into that possibility before you broadcast it?"

Silence again. Finally I said, "We're just kids, Mrs. Capelli."

"Yes." She nodded. Her voice was tighter. "You are children with unchecked access to a medium that is just too powerful . . . for children." She looked hard and quickly at Mr. Dallas.

Then Mrs. Capelli looked at Bethany's dad. She took a long breath.

"Mr. DeMere . . . I cannot tell you how very sorry we are

that this terribly unfortunate mistake has been made. We acknowledge, and very much regret, the pain it has caused your family. I want to thank you personally for bringing this very, *very* unfortunate matter to my attention. I can assure you, speaking personally and as the principal of this school, that I will see to it that nothing like this can ever happen again."

Bethany's dad stood up. "That doesn't undo the damage, Mrs. Capelli," he said. "My daughter is devastated. She doesn't know if she wants to come back to this school. She doesn't know if she can."

"I hope she will, Mr. DeMere," Mrs. Capelli said. "I very much hope she will come back to us. We will do everything we possibly can to make the truth known to everyone here. And, as I say, nothing like this will *ever* occur again."

He looked at her for a long time. Then he nodded. "We'll see how the situation unfolds, Mrs. Capelli."

She stood up; she held out her hand. He looked at it for a second before he decided to shake it.

He left.

Mrs. Capelli blew out air like she was expelling steam.

"Of all the foolish, dumb, reckless, idiotic things you could possibly have done. Do you have any idea the kind of trouble you have exposed us to?"

"I guess not really," I said.

"Lawyers don't just come into people's offices and talk like that," she said. "First they talk like that, then they *sue* people. And schools. For *lots* of money."

There was a pause. Elliot said, "Is that why this is so bad?"

"Mr. Gekewicz? I beg your pardon?"

"No, I mean, we're really sorry for what happened. We're *really* sorry. But, like, does this mean when kids get beat up or dropped off bridges, or people make up stories about *them*, the only reason you don't do anything is 'cause their dads aren't lawyers?"

She shot him a look. "This is not some kind of joke, Mr. Gekewicz."

"I totally agree with you."

She slapped her palm on the desk. Hard. "I take my responsibilities to this school very seriously. And you have created a very, very serious situation."

"We're sorry," Catalina croaked.

"It is now my responsibility to do everything I can, in a very public and visible manner, to make sure this can never happen again. Just as I said."

Mrs. Capelli looked at Mr. Dallas. "I am revoking student access to the SchoolStream network," she said.

He jerked forward like he'd been punched in the stomach. "Which students? These?"

"All students."

"*What?* Janet . . . no. That would be a terrible mistake. You've got no idea how much the kids use the LAN. How much they get out of it."

"The potential for abuse has been made very plain, Mr. Dallas. I have the responsibility to take decisive action. You just heard me promise I would."

He looked desperate. "Janet, the Technology Committee decided on these levels of access."

"With a great deal of pressure from its chairman." She glared at him.

"Yes. Because it was *right*," he said, and he started talking fast. "Because it's a tool for learning. It has limitless potential. Limitless. It's not that there won't be any mistakes—of course there will be mistakes. How many books have been published that maybe shouldn't have been? How many unfortunate phone calls get made every day? The point is, networked communication is the new world. Trusting kids to explore it and make sense of it is trusting them to *learn*. To learn its lessons."

Mrs. Capelli shook her head. Mr. Dallas spread his arm toward us.

"This is what's *really* happening here," he said. "Three kids make innovative use of the network. Really innovative. They start doing some real good, too. Then they make one mistake. One serious mistake—but still, just one mistake. They have a chance to learn from that. Everybody has a chance to. They can use the network to make it right, for gosh sakes. But if you take the network away from the whole student body because of this . . ."

Mrs. Capelli just glared. Mr. Dallas looked all around the room. He sagged, like he was losing air.

"I don't know what that says. I guess it tells people you shouldn't try something new, stick your neck out, or try to make a difference—because your boss might get a lawyer in her office."

Mrs. Capelli's face darkened. I jabbed Elliot. He elbowed me back.

"Open student access to this school's computer network is a loose cannon pointed at every single person in this school community," she said to Mr. D. "It is my responsibility to protect this institution from that kind of exposure. In view of what has happened, I am overruling the decision of the Technology Committee. Student access to SchoolStream is to be confined to retrieving information from the library and so forth. There will be no more electronic mail. No more bulletins. Effective immediately."

Mr. Dallas stood up. He just stood there, breathing loudly. Finally he said, "We can't do this immediately. The kids will need time to take it in. To wind it down."

Mrs. Capelli thought about that. "I don't see why, Mr. Dallas. But all right. You have two weeks.

"Now," she said to us three. "Let's talk about what you're going to do to make this better."

We had to write a letter of apology to Bethany, which killed me to do—and make a copy for her dad. We had to give the letters to Mrs. Capelli, so she could mail them with, no doubt, some fawning and scraping little note of her own.

We each got two weeks' detention. And we had to write a letter to the Parkland Middle School student body. We had to sign and print out a copy for every homeroom and deliver every one in person, so each teacher could copy it and give one to every single student the next morning. The letter had to say exactly what Mrs. Capelli wanted it to say. I said the best way would be to post it on the network—but there were not going to be any more postings on the network. Not by us. We were off KidNet, as of the end of the school day.

We went to the computer lab in activities block to write our letters. First we checked Elliot's e-mail. There were more messages waiting for us than ever before.

One miserable rainy day we got our grades. There was this kid Donnie (not his real name) who usually got pretty poor grades, but this time he got A's and B's. He went up to this guy Matt who always picked on him and he said, "Hey, look—I got better grades than you! I'm smarter than you!"

Well, that was stupid. Matt said, "You're a stupid loser—those are someone else's grades." Donnie said, "They are not—they're mine," but Matt said, "I think you're lying. Let me see."

Donnie held the report card away but it was too late—Matt grabbed it. He said, "I knew it. These aren't your grades. It's just a stupid mistake." And he went outside and threw the report card where the kindergarten kids were walking after school and they walked all over it. They tromped on it. They were laughing. When Donnie tried to get it back Matt dragged him behind the school and beat him up bad.

That's a true story.

One time when I was in elementary school at recess I really wanted to play kickball. But on the playground these two guys started calling me names and saying I was so spastic I couldn't play. I tried to ignore them and just start playing but they started saying it to all the other people. They said, "He can't play—he's too spastic, he can't kick or catch and when he runs he just falls down . . . Which I only did once. Now all the kids were saying, "Yeah, they're right, go away." I didn't want to tell on anybody and have everybody hate me even more, so I just went and sat on a swing till that recess was over.

i like pounding on kids for fun. Hey, try it sometime if you think it isn't fun. One time after school I felt like having some fun, so I got in the way of this other kid. I told her to get off the sidewalk, and I shoved her into a tree. She kicked me hard in the shins and ran, that little creep. It hurt! I went home MAD!

Some eighth graders were playing dodgeball in gym. They missed the ball and I went to get it for them. But one of the kids chased the ball and said to me I would be stabbed with a switchblade if I touched the ball. He used swears, too, like he really meant it. I did not touch anything.

There was this kid, a real mean-minded misfit, who was picking on me all year. He would call me weenie-boy and dick-face. One time he took my new basketball cards and ripped them up, and then he threw my whole binder of

156

cards into the storm sewer. I had hundreds of them, all in plastic sleeves, all arranged. I tried and tried to reach it with sticks but that was hopeless, it was ruined anyway. And I never did get it.

I used to feel so all alone because of this guy, like I could never be okay or have any friends again. Then when I started reading *The Revealer* I realized this stuff happened to a lot of kids in my grade (sixth). We had a discussion in English about it, and I made friends with two other kids. Now we stick together, and because we are together the troublemakers do not give us so much trouble anymore.

P.S. You can use my story.

TATER TOTS

At lunchtime we were still in shock. We sat there sort of poking at our food.

Elliot and I had the grilled cheese and Tater Tots. Catalina had a turkey sandwich from home. Finally, Elliot said, "So . . . does your dad make your lunch?"

She nodded sadly. "Yes. I mean, he does all right. But it's pretty all-American." She lifted up a corner of the bread, peered at the flap of turkey.

"No *merienda*," Elliot said.

She smiled. "You remembered."

"Sure."

We sat. We chewed.

"Who do you think did this?" Elliot said. "I mean, there must be a lot of people who don't like Bethany DeMere. But who really *hates* her? And who would be nasty enough to try something like this?"

"I hadn't thought about that," Catalina said.

"Well, obviously somebody really wanted to get her in trouble. That's why they gave us an anonymous disk—that's why the story didn't come in on KidNet, like all the others.

This way we couldn't find out who it came from. Even if we'd tried we couldn't have found out." He looked at me. "Right?"

I stared at the table.

"But now we *have* to figure it out—somehow," Elliot said. "I mean, if we can find out who really did this, maybe it won't be so totally bad for us." He looked at me again. "Right?"

"I did it," I said.

His eyes bugged. *"What?"*

"I mean, it's my fault. It's totally my fault. It's my stupid, stupid fault."

"What are you talking about?"

"She knew I would believe it, because she knew I'd read that essay. She knew I wanted to get her. And she knew I'm a stupid moron who has to screw *every*thing up."

With my fork I speared a Tater Tot. I lifted it, and looked at it. "This," I said, "is smarter than me."

"Wait a minute," Elliot said. "You think Bethany did this? To herself?"

"She didn't do it to herself. She did it to us."

Elliot squinched up his face and stared at his tray. Then he shook his head.

"I don't get it," he said.

"Well, I do. It was perfect. She makes it up, okay? She writes it and puts it on a disk, which she tapes to Catalina's locker. We know she knows about anonymous notes, and we know she knows which is Catalina's locker. We know she's evil, and she's not stupid. Her dad said she's always on the honor roll."

Elliot leaned forward on his elbows. "And she knows you'll believe the story, because it mentions the exact words of an essay that she knows you saw. Huh. Yeah. She knows we'll use the story, because . . ."

"Because she knows we hate her. *And* because she knows I'm stupid. I'm a loser. And I'm a moron."

"Uh . . . well."

"I don't hate her," Catalina said.

"No, no, you're both wonderful. It's me."

Elliot looked at Catalina. She peered sideways at me.

"So when the story does come out," Elliot says, "she goes to her dad."

"Who she knows is a lawyer."

He nods. "And she's unbelievably upset. Traumatized."

"Oh, totally."

"And of course she wails that her future is destroyed, unless . . ."

"Unless we are destroyed," Catalina said.

"And that's it," I said, pointing with the fork. "That's it. Checkmate. Two moves and we're done."

Catalina picked the Tater Tot off my fork. She bit off a tiny piece; her face pinched up. "Eew. You eat these things?"

Elliot speared two of his Tots, slid them with his teeth off his fork, and chewed. "They made me what I am today," he said. "These and Milk Duds."

I stood up. They looked up. Elliot said, "What?"

"I'm going back to Mrs. Capelli. I'm going to tell her it was all me."

"No, you're not. Don't be an idiot."

"I *am* an idiot, all right?" It came out loud, and they looked startled.

"You're not an idiot," Elliot said softly. "It was our mistake. We were all there. We all decided to use that story."

"You were off in the ozone," I said to Elliot. I pointed at Catalina: "And you didn't want to do it. It was me. No one else could be so . . . *stupid*."

My eyes watered up. I was still standing there.

Catalina put her hand on my arm.

"Please don't," she said. "Okay?"

I shook my head. "Do you realize how mad at us people are going to be? Do you realize what a disaster this is? I got KidNet taken away from the whole school. We're not just nobodies again—when people find out we're the reason this happened, *they are going to HATE us!*"

I said that really loud, and suddenly the whole cafeteria fell silent and everyone turned toward our corner as I said, "And it's my fault because *I am a TOTAL MORON!*"

Silence. Everyone was looking at me. Then everyone started to laugh.

I turned away. The rattling laughter swelled up behind me like a wave. I wouldn't look at anyone . . . I stalked stiff-legged out of there as fast as I could.

I was rushing down the hall. I was rushing to get away, not knowing where I could go that no one could find me . . . and I ran into Mr. Dallas. Oh, god. He came out the door of the System Server room, spotted me, and came rushing up. He was agitated.

"Hey, Russell," he said. "Hey, you look about as upset as I feel. Listen, I'm glad to see you. I really am. I wanted to talk to one of you guys."

I looked around. There wasn't any escape. He was a teacher.

"How about coming in here for just a second?" he said. "I'd like to talk to you. For just a second."

In his tiny room, he dumped himself backward into a rolling chair. I stood there against the erector-set wall.

He shook his head. "I can't believe this," he said. "This is supposed to be how you *learn*—by trying things, making mistakes and then dealing with them. Making things better. I mean, for god's sake." He folded his arms.

"I wonder if there's some way that we—well, I was thinking you guys—could somehow show people how important this system really is."

He shook his head again. "I know that sounds impossible. I mean, the system's shutting *down*. I know it is. When Janet Capelli makes a decision . . . let's just say she's not into changing her mind. But if there were some way to really demonstrate what this has meant to all these kids."

There was a heartbroken desperation in his eyes. I realized how much I had really done.

I just looked at him. I started to go.

"No," he said. "I realize it's not a practical idea. It's not an idea at all. That's the problem: I don't *have* an idea." He looked up. "Well, thanks, Russell. Thanks for talking this over with me."

I went out. And coming up the hall were Elliot and Catalina. They saw me and started walking toward me quickly. Elliot held up his hands.

"Hey, listen," he said, "we're sorry. We didn't laugh. We're sorry."

Mr. Dallas came out. "Mr. D," Elliot said, surprised.

"I was just talking with Russell about whether there was some way we could do something," Mr. D said, "to show how important KidNet really is to these kids. I mean, maybe all three of you could think about it. Do you think?"

"Well—" Elliot started to say.

"Leave me alone," I said.

Elliot said, "We just want to—"

"Just leave me out of it," I said. "Don't be stupid, all right? Try not to be so *stupid*."

I don't know what I meant. As usual, it was an idiotic, moronic, totally pointless thing to say.

I turned to walk away.

"Well, okay," Elliot said behind me. "If that's what you want, if that's how you're going to act. Then okay."

Nobody said anything more. I thought, That's it? Just like that? It's over?

I started walking fast.

I spent the rest of that day in a daze. I didn't think about anything, I just did what I had to do and didn't look at anybody, and I got out of there as soon as I could.

I walked up Chamber Street to the railroad tracks. I walked up onto the tracks and then out along them till I was way out of town. Finally I got off the tracks. I walked down a path, down a steep bank through ghostly white birch trees. I stumbled across a bumpy, tall-grass field to where the river was. I sat down by the water.

I just sat there. I was mad at everybody: at Bethany for being evil, her dad for being a tool, Mrs. Capelli for being authoritarian, Mr. Dallas for being a ditz, Elliot and Catalina for being hopeless, Burke and Blanchette for being mean, Richie for not seeing me today and beating the crap out of me, my mom for having to work all the time so she couldn't find me today and save me. My dad for dying, for god's sake. My dad for dying.

Finally, all that stuff drained away. It sort of washed down the river, I think. And I sat there knowing it all didn't matter, because it was really just me. It was just me. That's all. It was hopeless. *I* was hopeless.

I sat there for a long time. Then, it's funny, but I started hearing the river. The actual river. It has all these voices. They're interesting. There's a kind of whispering, and somebody else trying to say something, say something, and a louder voice talking over that—and then you realize it's all kinds of voices, all these different voices talking. It's really just a river . . . but it was interesting, and kind of funny, too. It cooled me down.

It was getting dark. I was hungry. I decided to go home.

That night I told my mom about the tape recorder. "It was all broken," I said. "Totally."

"That's okay. It was old. I never used it. The important thing is that *you're* all right."

I nodded. I didn't tell her anything else.

THE NATURAL ORDER

When I came in the next morning I saw a note taped to my locker door. I had a quick jolt of hope that it was from Elliot or Catalina. But when I unfolded it, I recognized the handwriting.

Hi there, Smart Boy—
Guess you got outsmarted, huh?

Under that someone else had written:

Yeah—welcome back to loserland. You messed with the wrong people!
signed, your friends (NOT)

I stuffed it in my pocket and went to homeroom, the last place on earth I wanted to be.

The short letter we had written the day before had been photocopied and put at everyone's place on the black lab tables. Nothing was said about it. Nothing. People just read the words Mrs. Capelli had told us we had to say:

Dear Fellow Students,

A story that was published on SchoolStream a few days ago, by us, was not true. This story said that a student had asked someone else to write some of her work. There was no truth to this story at all.

We are sorry for this mistake. It was a very serious mistake, and we apologize for making it.

> *Sincerely,*
> *Catalina Aarons*
> *Elliot Gekewicz*
> *Russell Trainor*

Kids read it and put it down and looked at each other. People whispered. Then most of them folded the paper up and put it in their notebooks. Or they just left it there.

Next to me, Chris Kuppel leaned over and whispered, "What happened?"

I shrugged.

"Well?" he said. "What?"

I didn't say anything. The black tabletop looked almost like reptile skin. Like it had scales. Then with a click and a quick whine, the PA system came on.

"Good morning, boys and girls," Mrs. Capelli said, like she always did. She read the morning announcements. Then she said, "Also today, boys and girls, we have a special announcement. Mr. Dallas would like to tell you about it. So I'm going to turn the microphone over to him."

There was a shuffling sound, then a man cleared his voice. "Ah . . . thank you. Yes. Good morning. This is—ahm, well, this is not actually an announcement I would like to tell you about at all. But it's my responsibility to tell you."

We could hear him take a deep breath.

"Owing to some . . . controversial use of the School-Stream system, I am sorry to say that as of two weeks from today, student use of the network will be restricted to the Library level of access. This will affect all students. This change—well, I'm sorry." He cleared his throat. "This change will be permanent."

There was a *thunk* as he shut off the microphone. In a few seconds there was a click and Mrs. Capelli came back on. She led us through the Pledge of Allegiance. But in our class the kids barely mumbled along. They were just staring at each other.

"Are they *serious*?" Big Chris whispered to me. There was a windstorm of whispering now, all over the room. A lot of people were turning to look at me, then turning away.

Chris held up our letter. He said, "These things are connected, aren't they?" I nodded.

"Well, geez, Russell, what *happened*?"

I pulled the note from my locker out of my pocket. I unfolded it and pushed it over to him.

He read it. He squinted at it.

"I don't get it," he said.

I shrugged. "We got set up."

He looked at me, then back at the note. "By who?"

I shrugged again.

Chris started studying the note, peering really closely at it. He kept looking at it. Finally he handed it back. I put it away. Chris sat back and crossed his arms. He looked really bothered.

"Man," he finally said. He shook his head. "That is just . . . *man*."

"I'd like to start today with a current-events discussion," Ms. Hogeboom said in social studies, coming around to perch on the front of her desk.

She looked around the room. "Just the other day, some of you were suggesting that if Anne Frank had had access to the Internet—if the world had been networked in those days, the way it is now—then maybe somehow she would have eluded her fate. I know you weren't sure about that, but it was definitely an interesting idea. Especially because you've had your own network in school this year."

There was shuffling and murmuring. There were a lot of frowns.

"Okay? People? Now, we all heard the announcement this morning. I can tell you it was as unexpected to me as I think it was to you. But I guess you're going to go to a restricted-access setup. I wonder what you think about that."

"We think it sucks," said Jake Messner loudly.

"Uh . . . Jake?"

"It's supposed to be a network for learning, and they're shutting out the students," he said. "What's *that* about?"

"Well . . . I can understand how you could see it that way," she said.

"It's not the administration's fault," Leah Sternberg piped up. "We had a meeting of the Student Council this morning."

"So whose fault is it?" Jake said.

"I think that's pretty clear."

"Not to me. Why don't you explain it to me?"

Leah sat up straight, hands folded on her desk. "A few students were abusing the system," she said. "There were stories of violence and . . . abuse against students being spread on the network. At least one of them was definitely untrue. We all know about that." She looked around for backup. I remembered how just a few days ago, Leah Sternberg was telling us how *The Revealer* was doing *so* much good for our school.

"A few students ruined it for everyone else," she said.

Bethany was sitting up front. She slightly, just slightly, rippled her hair.

"Well . . . I'm not looking to rub salt into anyone's wounds," Ms. Hogeboom said. "Maybe we shouldn't . . ."

"What if things aren't always the way they seem?"

Ms. Hogeboom looked puzzled. "Chris? What do you mean?"

Big Chris sat back. He rubbed his chin, and looked around.

"There are a couple of people in this class who know what I mean," he said. "Isn't that right, Bethany?"

Bethany looked straight ahead.

Chris said, "You know . . . I think maybe Burke would know, too. You know what I mean, Burke?"

Burke Brown shot a fast, dark look at Big Chris. Chris nodded. "I saw something you wrote, man. I know your handwriting." Chris smiled. He said, "I wonder what I might mean by that?"

I saw Burke sneak a look at Bethany. Then he saw me and glared back.

Ms. Hogeboom said, "Could we . . . could we please talk in terms that the whole class can follow?" She looked at Chris, at Burke, at Bethany. "Is this relevant to our discussion?"

Burke said, "No, 'cause it doesn't make any sense. Especially because some people don't know who their friends are. Or used to be."

There was a lot of murmuring.

"All right," Ms. Hogeboom said. "Why don't we . . ."

"I don't know what any of *that*'s about," said Allison Kukovna, "but I think this is a total tragedy for the whole school. I don't understand why one mistake should ruin it for everybody."

Elliot was looking down at his desk. Catalina's face had turned back to the mask. Neither of them looked at me.

"Well, that's life," said Jon Blanchette, and he grinned.

"Yeah," said a voice in the back. It was Turner.

"They've got us where they want us," he said. "That sure is life."

"Could this be the last comment before we move on?" Ms. Hogeboom said. "Turner, do you have a point to make?"

Turner shrugged. "This fake-story thing was an excuse to shut us off. Period. They never wanted us linked up to each other in the first place."

People were looking at him with baffled expressions.

"Oh sure, they'd like us to stay plugged in—by ourselves," Turner said. "But they don't want you *talking* to each other. They don't want you telling your stories. Oh sure, it's fine if it's on television. But not the *real* stories."

"Well, this is interesting," Ms. Hogeboom said.

"We're teenagers now, okay?" Turner said. "From now on they don't want to hear from us. You watch. If we do regular teenager things, and get in regular teenager trouble now and then, they'll *worry* about us. They love to do that. And they'll complain about us, of course. But if we start telling people the truth, if we say things they don't want people to hear, they will do everything they can to shut us up. They'll shut us out. They'll take us off the *network*."

Turner sat back, and shrugged. "Yeah. That's life all right."

"But," Ms. Hogeboom said, "the school invested thousands of dollars in this network."

"Yeah," said Jake, "until we started *using* it. So now we'll only be able to get stuff on the system that the school wants us to get."

"Like homework assignments," said Allison, nodding.

"And stuff from the library," said Chris.

"Well. A lot of materials, actually," Ms. Hogeboom said.

"Oh sure," Jake said. "We just won't be able to talk to each other. What's *that* about?"

"Oh, come on—we talk to each other all the time," said Leah Sternberg. "We are not like hiding in secret annexes. We have telephones, we have computers, we still have the Internet. We have plenty of choices."

"But this one was a little too powerful," Jake said.

"It was too connected," Turner added from the back. "Look, they've got a brand-new CD-rewritable machine in the computer lab. You can put 640 megs of multimedia on a disk—words, pictures, sound, video, whatever you want. They *want* you to use that. Just as long as you stay plugged in by yourself. See, that's safe. It's like a glorified Game Boy."

The class didn't say anything. Finally, Ms. Hogeboom said, "Well, I think that's a very challenging viewpoint. And I don't mean to cut things off, but I think that's a good place to stop. We still have twenty minutes, and I happen to have this twenty-minute historic film about Amsterdam and the legacy of Anne Frank. If someone could just get the lights— wait, let me plug this in. Okay. Lights?"

And then we had darkness, and the old, flickering black and white.

In the hall after class, Bethany and Burke were together. She whispered something to him. He looked up to see me.

"Hey, smart boy," Burke said. "What you got to say now?"

I didn't say anything.

"Gee," said Burke, "I don't see your tough-guy friend any- where. Do I? Actually, I don't see your weenie friends either. Where'd all your friends go, smart boy?"

Bethany was behind him, smirking at me.

"Don't have much to say, huh?" Burke said. "Well, you know what? Neither do I. I just want to make sure you un- derstand that you are right back where you belong, you and your friends. *If* they're still your friends."

He stood in my way. "This is the natural order, kid," he said. "You're on the bottom—and this time, you are going to stay there."

He stepped away. Bethany started walking down the hall with him. He said something to her and she laughed.

At lunchtime, Catalina was sitting with Allison and her friends at their table, in the middle of everything. Elliot was at our old table with Big Chris Kuppel. I could hardly believe it. Elliot looked up when he saw me, but I walked away. I went and ate my lunch by myself.

THE DUMPSTER

In afternoon detention we weren't allowed to talk, which was fine with me. Catalina did homework. Elliot sat and read a dinosaur book. I did nothing. Detention was in Ms. Hogeboom's room that day and I looked at stuff on the walls, stuff I'd read a million times before and never paid much attention to. Like the banner above the blackboard that said, in big letters: NEVER SETTLE FOR LESS THAN YOUR BEST. Uh-huh. There was also a poster for Mr. Dallas's Creative Science Fair. And there was a section of the bulletin board that was crowded with political cartoons, headlines, pictures of people in the news. Above that stuff more big letters said: WHEN YOU BELIEVE IN YOUR-SELF, ANYTHING IS POSSIBLE.

Nice try, Ms. Hogeboom.

When three forty-five came, I hadn't done a thing. Ms. Hogeboom said we could go. Elliot and Catalina picked up their stuff and left.

Ms. Hogeboom was looking at me.

"Russell," she said, "I imagine this has been a tough couple of days for you." I started gathering up my stuff. She said, "I wouldn't be surprised or blame you if you were upset. I just wonder if you'd like to talk about it."

I shook my head.

"It's okay if you talk about it," Ms. Hogeboom said gently.

I didn't want to. But then I heard myself whisper, "It's . . . just over. That's all."

"What?" she said. "What's over?"

I shrugged. "Everything. We got beat. We are beat." I zipped the backpack. I couldn't say any more.

She came around and sat on her desk. "Why?"

I couldn't answer.

"Why are you beat?" she said.

I shook my head. I didn't want to have this conversation. I was looking past her, at Mr. Dallas's poster.

A *"Little Bit More Challenging" Science Fair*, it said. The fair was in four weeks, the poster said. So what?

"I know this decision about the network was a disappointment," Ms. Hogeboom was saying. "And I know you feel responsible."

I did not want to hear this. I read the poster instead.

"But who says you have to be beaten?" she was saying.

The poster said, *The Challenge: Create something that tests an original hypothesis.*

"*Beaten*—that means ground down, doesn't it? Defeated. Depleted. Pretty much used up. Are you really used up? Russell? Russell, could you look at me?"

She was leaning sideways to catch my eye. "You're just beginning your life," she said. "Why should you feel used up?"

I didn't answer.

"May I tell you what I've seen?" she said. "I've seen three promising kids who had each been unconfident, unsure—in fact, isolated. Definitely. And so they got picked on. This happens, I know. It breaks my heart, but I see it all the time.

I see that it happens when young people have, among their peers, a lack of stature.

"But then these three kids got together. That was a big thing, wasn't it? Just that they got together. I saw that. And you know what? That made other things possible."

The poster said, *What do we mean, "original"?*

"These three kids started doing something," Ms. Hogeboom was saying. "They started to share their experiences. And they found a way to put those experiences in front of every student in the seventh grade."

"The whole school," I said.

"Pardon?"

"We put them in front of every kid in the school."

"Oh. Well, that's even better."

We mean YOU thought of it, the poster said. *The more unique, the better.*

"Anyway, the next thing anybody knew, other kids were sending in their stories," Ms. Hogeboom was saying. "Everybody was reading these stories, and something very subtle was beginning to happen. Just in the atmosphere of the school. I don't know how to put it, exactly . . ."

What do we mean, "create"? the poster said.

Ms. Hogeboom snapped her fingers. "Here's what I think it was. A lot of the time middle-schoolers are not very compassionate toward each other—especially to those who don't have stature. But all of a sudden I saw a humanizing. I think students were starting to look at each other a little bit differently. It was like a small revolution."

She smiled.

"Maybe that's a bit much," she said. "But I really felt that students were actually starting to treat each other differently."

We mean when you're done, the poster said, *something exists that didn't exist before.*

"And now you three had stature," Ms. Hogeboom was saying. "You were making an impact every day. You actually had power, all of a sudden. Maybe that didn't please everyone—maybe it even made some people nervous. Maybe they wanted to stop you, or knock you down. Or maybe you just made a mistake. I don't really know. But meanwhile, this other thing, this more general humanizing thing, *has* been happening.

"If you let yourself be beat, Russell," she said. "Russell? Hello?"

I sat up. I still wasn't looking at her.

"If you are defeated," she said, "I wonder—will this other thing be defeated, too? Will some kids go right back to victimizing other kids, with that same old arrogance and impunity? Will everyone else go right back to not really seeing, and not really caring? Will my heart start to get broken again?"

Note: the poster said, *This fair will be judged by real scientists and technology professionals. Advance human knowledge! MAKE something—whether weirdly wacky or totally technical—that opens people's eyes!*

"Russell? Hello?"

"Huh?"

Ms. Hogeboom sighed.

"I guess you better go, Russell. Is someone here to pick you up?"

"No. I walk home."

"All right." She stood up. She thought for a second. Then she reached back on her desk, picked up a book, and tossed it to me. I missed it, and it fell to the floor. I picked it up.

It was her copy of Anne Frank's *Diary*. It still had that Mohawk shag of yellow Post-its across the top. The book had been read and reread and used so much that its cover had all these white cracks, its corners were rounded and swollen, and the spine had totally come apart. She had tape holding it together.

"I would say nobody is truly isolated unless they cut *themselves* off, Russell," she said. She nodded at Anne Frank's book in my hands. "That is one choice she never made."

Ms. Hogeboom held out her hand. I put the book in it.

"And now we have something we never had before," she said. "We have this."

Walking up Chamber Street and then through the parking lot, I was almost hoping the dark figure would be there. When I saw him leaning against the white wall of Convenience Farms, I was almost glad.

I came walking up. He nodded. "Hey."

"Hey."

I leaned up alongside him. I just stood there. I could feel him glance over at me.

"I read that letter," he said. "I heard what happened."

I looked down. "It was a setup," I said. "We got played."

"Yeah? By who?"

"Couple of kids."

"Huh. So, what are you gonna do about it?"

I scratched my foot in the gravel. "What *can* we do about it? We lost."

Richie stood out from the wall.

"Says who?"

"I don't know."

"Says you. Right? Says *you*."

"No, the kids who played us. They said things are meant to be this way. I mean, the principal said it."

"Oh, so that's it? A couple dirtball kids and that hot-air bag say you're done, so you're *done*?"

"Well what else can we do?" I was getting mad. "There's nothing we can do, all right?"

"No. That's not all right." He was staring at the ground. Then he looked right at me. "You're just gonna cave? I mean, you stand up to me, then a couple midgets trip you up and you're gonna *lie* there?"

"I don't know what to do!" I was yelling. "All right? Everybody thinks it was our fault!"

He shook his head. "I don't. So that's not everybody. Right? That's a *big* not everybody."

I shrugged.

"So," Richie said, "now you figure out how to clue in everybody else. What's so hard about that?"

"For the last time, Richie, I don't know what to do!"

He started looking around. He nodded. "Okay," he said. "See that thing over there?" He was pointing toward the back.

"The phone booth?"

"*No*, not the phone booth. There."

"The Dumpster?"

"Yeah. The Dumpster. You cave now, you give up now, where's the rest of your life going? Any guesses?"

"But I don't . . ."

"You don't always have to know what to do! You just have to know who you *are*. So who are you? Huh?"

He shoved me. Backward.

"Don't push me," I said. "I've had a bad day."

"I'm gonna push you right in that damn Dumpster. You want to go there, I'm gonna *put* you there."

"Don't."

"Why not? You're just gonna take it, right?" He pushed me again. I stumbled back. He pushed me *again*.

I stopped stumbling and launched myself at him. I shoved him in the chest, right in his stupid black jacket. He stumbled backward himself.

"You're just a damn bully, you know that? You think every

answer is just to shove someone around. It's not that simple, Richie, all right? It's not that easy!"

I stuck my face in Richie's. His eyebrows lifted, but that's all. I said, "I can't solve an incredibly complicated problem just because you act like a tough guy and tell me *or else*! I mean, or else what?"

Slowly, Richie turned up his open palms.

"Or else nothing, man. That's just it. Or else you got nothing."

I turned and walked away. But my mind was working—I will say that. All day I'd been numb and dumb and feeling stuck. But Richie got me thinking again.

That night I was so tired, I went to bed early. Then, when I was almost asleep, I sat straight up in bed.

I was wide awake. There in the dark, all the pieces came together, and I got it.

I *got* it!

In that instant, I knew what we could do.

DOUBLE CLICKS

✳ "So what's this?" said Jake Messner.

"Take a look," said Elliot, sliding the mouse his way.

We three watched as Jake slipped into a chair and double-clicked. He leaned forward and looked at the screen, while behind him dozens of other kids milled around the gym.

A big yellow banner on the wall above the blue hanging mats said, WELCOME TO THE CREATIVE SCIENCE FAIR! There was a buzz of noise and a bubbling-up of laughter as all the kids who'd just been let in circled the gym, eyeing the exhibits as they shuffled by and peered from safe distances, cracking smart comments from their little moving groups but usually, unlike Jake, too self-conscious to be the first to stop and actually look.

The three of us had already wandered around. Because our exhibit was easy to set up—just a computer and a simple sign—we'd had time to make the circuit before the general student body was admitted. Some of the projects were fairly funny, like "The Answer Guys." That was a refrigerator box three eighth-graders had painted silver, with an opening the shape of a TV screen cut out at face level. Below the "screen" was a button and a sign that said PUSH—THEN ASK ANY QUESTION.

When you pushed, a guy popped up, and no matter what you asked, he would loudly intone a serious-sounding answer. Then another kid at a table asked you to fill out a survey, which had only one question: "Did you believe your answer?" Every exhibit had to be based on a hypothesis, and this one's was: "A majority of people will believe you if you sound like you know what you're talking about."

Three sixth-graders had mummified a pig. They had used "ancient Egyptian methods," according to a pretty cool brochure they had created on the computer with their picture (not the pig's) on the cover, "to reconstruct the art of mummification." It was a prenatal pig, actually—unborn, but real. The brochure explained their methods: filling the "body cavities" with salt, soaking the body in baking soda, and filling the gut area with herbs mixed with Calvin Klein cologne. Their hypothesis was that mummification worked, but I figured they'd need to keep the pig around for a few years to know for sure.

Then there was "The Class Gas-O-Meter." This was a Plexiglas box containing a carbon-dioxide meter that was connected to a buzzer alarm. The hypothesis was that high levels of CO_2 ("Human Exhaust," the explanation panel explained) in school classrooms are "at least partially responsible for general discomfort, drowsiness, and increased perception of body odor experienced in school." The kids had tested several classrooms. They had a chart showing their results—which were that three out of five classes tested above the maximum CO_2 level set by the state, which was 1,000 parts per million.

That was probably the coolest exhibit, next to ours.

There was also "The Hamster Trainer Maze." This was one of those wooden skittle mazes where you spin a top and hope it makes it through several openings in the little walls to the goal. Only these kids had put a blob of peanut butter at the goal, and they kept letting a hamster go where you usually start the top. Their hypothesis was that you could train a hamster to find peanut butter in a maze. So far, though, they hadn't. I don't think they really got the idea of creating something new.

There were about a dozen other exhibits. Right in the middle was us.

Behind Jake, the tide of kids started to slow down. Some kids were stopping to look as our welcome screen swam up on the monitor:

Welcome to The Bully Lab
An Interactive Scientific Investigation

Created and assembled by: Catalina Aarons, Elliot Gekewicz, and Russell Trainor

School survey conducted and report written and narrated by: Catalina Aarons and Allison Kukovna

Reenactments featuring: Jon Blanchette, Elliot Gekewicz, Christopher Kuppel, and Richard C. Tucker

Interviews conducted by: Russell Trainor

Direction and videography by: Turner White

Project adviser: Claire Hogeboom

Technical adviser: Jerome Dallas

True stories contributed by: 42 students of Parkland Middle School

Stories collected via: Parkland School Local Area Network (LAN), running SchoolStream 3.0 communication software, with (formerly) open student access

<Go to Menu>

Jake clicked up the menu:

I. Hypothesis
II. Research Methods
III. Research Report
IV. Video Reenactments
V. Video Interviews
VI. Gallery of Nasty Notes
VII. The Stories

Turner White came up and leaned against the table, watching. He was wearing a black turtleneck, and an actual black beret.

"Try the hypothesis first," Catalina suggested.

"I want to see these reenactments," Jake said, quickly double-clicking.

Turner smiled as the titles came up:

A. *The Bus:* Chris & Elliot
B. *The Locker:* Jon & Elliot
C. *The Lunchroom:* Chris & Elliot
D. *The Playground:* Chris, Jon & Elliot
E. *In Your Face:* Richard

A small crowd of kids were now peering over Jake's shoulder. "Do *The Bus*," someone said. Jake nodded, and clicked.

The video window came up. Turner and Elliot and I had filled the back part of a school bus with a bunch of kids, so that it looked like the whole bus was full. It looked pretty good.

The kids are swaying back and forth like the bus is moving.

Elliot comes up the aisle. Only one seat is open—beside Chris.

Elliot puts his backpack on the floor, and turns to sit.

"You can't sit here."

"But it's the only seat left."

"It's *saved*."

"For who?"

"For anybody but you," Big Chris sneers. He slowly stands up. "You got a problem with that, shrimp-o?"

More kids, drawn by the video, joined the cluster around the computer.

"Well, yeah," Elliot says. "I need to sit *some*where."

He swings his butt and starts to sit—but Chris lowers his big shoulder and slams Elliot into the seat across the aisle so hard that Elliot goes sprawling over the two kids sitting there.

Chris picks up Elliot's backpack. He opens the bus window.

"Hey!" Elliot yells. The kids in the seats all laugh. Chris unzips the backpack and empties it out the window. Then he looks back, and grins.

The End
<Go to Menu>

"This," said Jake, grinning, "is cool."

"Yo, man, give someone else a chance!"

There was a crowd now, pushing and squeezing up behind his chair.

"There oughta be more than one station for this," somebody complained. I looked at Elliot, who shrugged.

"I'm next—I helped," Allison Kukovna said. Jake lifted up so she could slide in and nobody else. She gave him a little nudge. Elliot jabbed me, and I thought, *Hmmm*.

Allison punched up Research Methods:

To test our hypothesis, we distributed a special survey to every student in Parkland Middle School.

Allison's recorded voice reads the same words out loud.
"Boring," said someone in the crowd.
"Yeah—do more scenes," said someone else.
"Hey," Allison said, "I'm *narrating* here." Jake turned back and glared. The kids shut up.

Our questions were simple:
1. Have you ever been directly involved in a bullying or harassment incident at this school?
2. If "yes," were you:
   a. On the giver side?
   b. On the receiver side?
3. Have you been involved in more than 5 incidents?
4. More than 10?
5. Did you read *The Revealer* on SchoolStream?
6. Do you think that bullying and harassment in school have decreased since before *The Revealer*?

To see the responses and our analysis, click here for Research Report.
Click here to go back to Menu.

"Go to Menu!"
"Yeah!"
Allison nodded, and did. Kids were actually shouting.
"Interviews!"

"Reenactments!"

"I want to see the stories," someone said.

"Hey, we've *seen* the stories," said another kid. "They were on KidNet."

"Not all of them," Catalina piped up. "We collected lots more."

"How'd you do that?" Leah Sternberg asked, worming through the crowd. "Your access was revoked."

Elliot smiled at me. "We had help," he said.

Leah's forehead wrinkled, as if she was frustrated. Over her head came a big, thick hand, then Big Chris's head and shoulders. Elliot stood up far enough to slap hands.

"Like I said," he told Leah.

"You weren't supposed to."

"It was completely legal. We had two weeks before everyone *else* got shut down."

"I, myself," said Big Chris, "gained valuable computer networking, as well as acting, experience." He bowed.

"Would you like a turn?" Allison said to Leah. They did the butt-to-butt seat exchange.

Leah quickly opened Video Interviews.

A. Bethany DeMere and Catalina Aarons
B. Jon Blanchette, Burke Brown, and Elliot Gekewicz
C. Judith Lefkowitz, Guidance Counselor
D. Janet Capelli, Principal

Leah tapped keys. Up swam Mrs. Capelli, sitting on a chair. The crowd behind us groaned. "Not *her*," somebody said. Leah sat up straighter, and doubled-clicked.

"Mrs. Capelli," says the voice of the interviewer (me), "how much of a problem do you think bullying is at our school?"

"I don't know what you mean by *problem*," she says. "Are you suggesting it's uncontrolled?"

"I'm just asking how often you think it happens."

She shrugs. "Of course it does happen. It happens at all schools."

"Well, do you think it happens a lot at this school?"

She shakes her head. "What you might call 'bullying' can encompass a wide spectrum of quite typical preadolescent and adolescent behaviors. If two students get into an argument on the soccer field, and one happens to be bigger than the other, is that bullying? If a group of friends decide to exclude one member for a brief time, as so often happens at the middle-school age levels, unfortunately, is that bullying?"

"I think we mean when one person intentionally hurts or humiliates another person," I say.

"As I've said, this tends to occur at all schools—especially middle schools, unfortunately. As an educator, I don't wish to stereotype any of our students. But when specific incidents do occur, we are aggressive in our response to inappropriate behavior."

She folds her hands in her lap.

"Well . . . Mrs. Capelli, what do you think about this project?"

Now she leans forward. Her hands grip the chair.

"While I commend any responsible project for the science fair, I'm much less comfortable with something that seeks to deliberately humiliate certain people. Isn't that what *you* call bullying, Mr. Trainor? Mr. White?"

"Deliberately humiliating who, Mrs. Capelli?"

"I believe it's *whom*, Mr. Trainor."

"Okay. Deliberately humiliating whom?"

"Why, these young people whose stories you are featuring. Of course."

"But they've all given permission. We asked every one. They *wanted* to tell their stories."

"I'm very concerned that you are deliberately portraying Parkland School in a very one-sided, negative light," the principal says quickly. "What if you should win this science fair and go on to the district competition? How will that reflect on Parkland School? That we're somehow the capital of . . . cruelty?"

"We're just being honest. Aren't we?"

"I think this is just a way of victimizing some people you'd like to get back at," Mrs. Capelli says, pointing her finger at the camera. "I'm upset about it and it will *not* convince me to restore student access to SchoolStream, just in case that's what you're hoping will happen. I think you're only proving that students—that some students—can't be trusted to . . . to . . ."

She stops. Collects herself. Suddenly she smiles broadly at the camera.

"Well. I hope this has been a helpful interview."

"Whoa," somebody says.

"Go back to the fight scenes."

"They're *bullying* scenes, fathead."

"Hey, you call me that again . . ."

The crowd was growing even bigger and noisier. Everyone was demanding this and that—the scenes, the stories. I didn't know if anyone was at any of the other exhibits anymore. I couldn't see beyond our throng.

"What's on that screen—*WrestleMania*?" said a booming voice, coming through the crowd.

"Hey, Mr. Dallas," Elliot said.

"Elliot," he said, "you're a hit."

"Yeah. We need more computers!"

"Well, we only made the one CD, at least for now," he

said. "Who knew you'd draw a crowd like this? What do they want to see?"

"Mostly the videos."

"So give them a video!"

As the crowd pressed in around us, Elliot went back to the Video Interviews menu and punched up Bethany DeMere and Catalina Aarons. Catalina made a feeble effort to grab the mouse and choose something else, but then she sat back.

Mr. Dallas leaned over to me.

"Any glitches?" he whispered.

"None so far."

"Great. 'Cause after school is when the judges come through. With the principal."

He clapped me on the shoulder and backed away in the crowd. Mr. Dallas hadn't seen the interview with Mrs. Capelli—I hadn't had the nerve to show him. Mrs. Capelli hadn't seen anything. I knew the kids would like our project, though I also hadn't expected a crowd like this; but I wasn't at all sure what would happen when a bunch of grownups, including the principal, saw the scenes and interviews, especially this one:

Bethany and Catalina are sitting in chairs. Bethany is styling her hair with her fingers, then she sees the camera is on her. She lowers her head and smiles.

"Bethany," Catalina says. Bethany ignores her.

"Bethany."

"What?"

"Why did you make things up about me?"

"What?"

"Why did you make up stories that weren't true about me, and about my family and where I come from?"

"I never did that," Bethany says to the camera. "You're hallucinating."

"Actually, you did do that. You also made up the story that said you were cheating."

"What? You're *crazy*."

"Am I?"

Catalina picks up her backpack. She zips open the front pocket and pulls out a note. "You wrote this note to Russell Trainor. You taped it on his locker."

"No, I didn't."

"It says, *Hi there, Smart Boy—Guess you got outsmarted, huh?*"

Catalina says, "That was taped to Russell's locker *before* the student body came in and read our letter, saying the story we'd published about your cheating wasn't true. Whoever wrote this note knew that story was a fake. At that point, no other students—except the ones your father interviewed, who were all your friends—knew anything about the story being fake. At that exact point, only the students who actually planted that story would have known to say we had been outsmarted."

Bethany smiles at the camera. "That's ridiculous," she says. "And anyway, you can't prove I wrote that note."

"Here's another of your notes," Catalina says. "You wrote this one and dropped it in my locker."

"Yeah. Right." But Bethany is trying to peer at the note as Catalina unfolds it.

Catalina reads: *Everybody knows why the weird girl had to leave where she came from. Because she was so EASY the boys wouldn't even look at her in public anymore. She learned it from her mother . . .*

"That one was pretty horrible, Bethany. It wasn't true at all."

"I never wrote that! I didn't write either one of those." Bethany turns her hurt-looking face to the camera.

"But you did, Bethany. You wrote this one, too."

Catalina reaches in again, unfolds, and reads: *I'm not talking to you ANYMORE. I don't care WHAT happens.*

"You wrote that to Russell in social studies class," Catalina says. "You wrote it in front of him, and you handed it to him and he kept it. He kept all these notes. They're all in the same handwriting, Bethany. They're all yours. You made up the story that you cheated, just so we would publish it and get in trouble."

Bethany is stunned for just one second. Then she turns to the camera and cocks her head with an innocent expression.

"You know, my father's an attorney," she says nicely. "I think you've met him, haven't you?"

Catalina nods. "Yes, I did," she says. "Actually, we talked to a lawyer, too—a good friend of my dad's. He said we've got solid evidence, and if anybody has a case for slandering someone's reputation, it would be me. Against you."

Bethany crosses her arms. She doesn't say anything.

"I still don't understand why you'd want to hurt somebody that way," Catalina says. "But I finally decided if I let you get away with it, you'll think nobody will ever stand up to you. You'll think you can control everything. I realized it was worth taking a risk to prove what's really true. So if you'd like to talk to your dad, we think you should. In fact, here are the notes."

Catalina hands her the papers. Bethany looks wide-eyed for a second, then grabs them and gives the camera an amazed expression, as if she can't believe we're that dumb after all.

"Of course, those are photocopies," Catalina says. "We kept the originals. We even scanned them. They're on this CD—in the Gallery of Nasty Notes."

Bethany stares for a second at the papers in her hand. Then she turns to the camera. She inclines her head with a patient expression.

"Turner," she says softly, nicely, "I think you should give me the tape now, Turner. Come on, Turner. I'm stronger than you and you know it. Turner . . . give me the tape."

Bethany gets up from her chair. The camera backs up.

"Turner, take the tape out and give it to me. Come *on*."

Bethany's walking forward; the camera moves jerkily back.

"Give me the *tape*, Turner!"

She rushes for him and the whole image tilts, and then there's snow and noise. And that's it.

The crowd around our monitor erupted in a swirl of talk. Jake said in my ear, "What happened? Did she get the tape?"

"It's a new digital camera—only Turner knows how to work it," I said. "She grabbed it and shook it a little, then she handed it back and stormed off."

Jake grinned. "Huh!" Then he frowned. "But aren't you scared she'll get her dad to sue you? Didn't he already say he might?"

I shrugged. "If you were Bethany, would you want your dad to see this? And even if he did see it, would he want a lot more people to know she did this? I mean, we have the evidence."

"I guess so," he said. "So what about when the principal sees it?"

"Uh, well . . ." I felt a familiar prickle of fear. "That part I'm not too sure about."

REFLECTED GLORY

"Well, that was fun," I said as the last classes crowded back out the gym doors.

"Yeah," said Elliot. "The network's still history, though. You heard what she said."

"So we can't do miracles. At least we won't be outcasts with the kids."

Elliot smiled. "Not anymore."

It was quiet in the gym. We could finally take a break. It was two-thirty; school got out at two forty-five, but we had to stay here and wait for the judges to come at three. After that we got to go home for dinner—then we had to be back when the parents came to see the fair at seven.

"I bet Bethany tells her dad there's nothing interesting at the science fair," Elliot said.

"Oh, yeah. He wouldn't want to see any of *this* stuff."

Catalina punched Eject on the CD drive and the tray slid out. She lifted the shiny disk by its edges. It was silver-blue as she tilted it, holding it up to the light. Then she slid it back in. Her fingernails were painted with silver sparkles.

"Well, these last four weeks were definitely fun," Elliot said.

"Yeah."

"We might even win the science fair," Catalina said.

Elliot and I both shrugged. After all, that was never really the point.

The judges were a tall woman in a white lab coat with a hospital name tag that said MEDICAL TECHNOLOGIST, a burly guy with a beard and a heavy purple shirt who looked like a mountain man but who they said was a software developer, and a man in a suit who was looking bright-eyed at everything. Mr. Dallas and Ms. Hogeboom were there, too. Mrs. Capelli was fluttering around the man in the suit.

"Children, this is Dr. David Bennett, the chair of our school board," she said.

We shook the man's hand and also the others'. Dr. Bennett—I never found out if he was a medical doctor or some kind of scientist—had sandy hair and a roundish, open face, almost like a little kid's, and a quick, happy smile. When we punched up the main menu, he slid eagerly onto the chair between Catalina and me.

"So let's see this," he said. "'The Bully Lab,' in multimedia. Well, isn't *this* unusual. Hmm . . . okay. The hypothesis." He double-clicked. Allison's voice came on again:

"Our hypothesis is that bringing bullying and harassment incidents to light among the whole student body in a school will result in these incidents happening less often, and being less severe."

Dr. Bennett whistled. "Now that's a hypothesis," he said. He leaned back. "Grady? Sharon? Any thoughts?"

"I'd love to see the proof," the lab-coat lady said.

"Click on," said the mountain man.

Dr. Bennett pulled up Research Methods and read the list of questions. Nodding, looking interested, he brought up Research Report. He clicked on Audio Text.

Catalina's voice came up, alternating with Allison's:

"We distributed our survey to all students, and received an eighty-five-percent response," Catalina says. "This seemed like an incredible response. We think it showed a lot of interest and support for our project."

"Out of the three hundred forty-three surveys we received back," says Allison, "two hundred thirty students—sixty-seven percent—said they had been involved in a bullying or harassment incident at our school. Seventy-four percent of those students said they had been on the victim side. Twenty percent had been on the bullying side. Six percent did not answer this question."

"Forty-eight percent of the students said they had been involved in more than five incidents," says Catalina's voice. "Twenty-three percent said they had been involved in more than ten."

I looked back. Mrs. Capelli's face was stiff. Her eyes flicked from the school board chairman to the screen.

"Our final results were these," Allison says. "Ninety-two percent of the students who responded said they had read *The Revealer* on the SchoolStream network. *The Revealer* was an electronic publication that gave kids a chance to tell their own stories of bullying.

"Eighty-two percent of the students who responded to our survey," says Catalina, "felt bullying had decreased in our school since *The Revealer* was first published."

Dr. Bennett broke into a wide smile. "Eighty-two *percent*," he said, turning back to the other grownups. "And you have this *Revealer* on the school system?"

"We had it," Catalina said.

His forehead crinkled for just a second. Then he said, "So . . . what was in it?"

"Click on The Stories," Elliot said.

He did. For a good five or ten quiet minutes, the judges read story after story.

"And these are all true?" said the mountain man, in a quiet voice.

"Kids sent them in," I said. "We got everyone's permission to include their stories."

"Not at *first*," Mrs. Capelli said.

"But we learned," said Elliot.

"These three students conceived, directed, and coordinated the project," Ms. Hogeboom piped up. "But they were helped by literally dozens of others. Not only the additional students who are credited on the menu, but also, what was it—forty-six?"

"Forty-two," I said.

"Forty-two students contributed their own stories," she said.

"Forty-two out of more than four hundred," Mrs. Capelli pointed out.

"That's *very* impressive," Dr. Bennett said.

The principal made a sound like a strangled duck.

"We didn't do this to make the school look bad," Elliot said. "We did it because this stuff happens."

"Well, of course—you're social scientists," Dr. Bennett said. "I want to see more. What else is good?"

"Try the interviews," I said, and he clicked up this one:

"Hey, Elliot, it was all just for fun. You know that," says
Jon Blanchette. He, Elliot, and Burke sit on three plastic chairs.

"Yeah—until you dumped your lunch on me in the cafeteria," Burke says. "That wasn't fun. I got you back, though, didn't I?"

"Did you?" Elliot says.

Burke smiles. "Maybe I did."

Elliot shakes his head. "You're the weird one, Burke. You know that? You guys thought it was so much fun to wait for me before school, after school, on the playground, in the halls, just so you could do something nasty. I mean, you hung my backpack in a tree, you played soccer with my lunch. You even dropped me off a bridge."

"*You* did that," Burke says. "We were only teaching you a lesson. The guys never would have dropped you if you'd just held still."

"But what was all that about?" says my voice, off camera. "Why do all that stuff to one particular kid?"

"Hey, we were just having fun," says Blanchette. "You *liked* it," he adds, grinning at Elliot.

"You think I liked it?"

"You definitely liked it. You could have avoided us. You never did. Right? It was part of your day, too. We were the guys who paid attention to you, Elliot. Weren't we?"

Elliot is shaking his head, but he's smiling, too.

"Calling me Geekowitz."

"At least we called you something," Jon says. "I mean, weren't we the only ones?"

"Nah, there were lots. You were just the nastiest."

"Now you're talkin'," Blanchette says, leaning back and giving the camera his big natural smile.

Next, Dr. Bennett clicked up Richie—and suddenly he was in your face, filling the camera.

"What are YOU looking at?"

Dr. Bennett's head jerked back. I glanced around. Mrs. Capelli looked paralyzed, and everyone was staring at the screen.

Richie's face was darkly angry. That was our idea, his and mine: to show you what it's like.

"Hey. You." He points with his chin. "Why are you looking at me?"

"I wasn't," my voice says.

His eyebrows clench and his head tilts. He speaks softly, as if he's puzzled: "Are you calling me"—the eyebrows lift—"a liar?"

"No! I didn't mean to."

"Oh, *please*," he simpers in his baby voice. "I *didn't mean to*." He looks you up and down. He smirks, and doesn't say anything. Finally he leans even closer, and whispers, "You know what I'm going to do to you?"

He nods, with the slightest smile.

"You don't know, do you? And you don't know when . . . *do* you? Might be in the bathroom. Might be after school. Might be almost anyplace where no one's watching."

He raises those eyebrows again, like now you and he have a secret. "I might be . . . *anywhere*."

He slowly smiles. But his eyes stay hard.

"See ya," he says, and the screen goes blank.

The grownups were totally silent. For a long time, no one said anything. Finally, Dr. Bennett almost whispered, "That was powerful."

"A remarkable actor," said the lady judge.

"I don't think he was acting," said the mountain man.

"Perhaps not," Dr. Bennett murmured.

Another pause.

"Tell me," the school board chairman finally said, turning to us. "How did this project get started?"

We three looked at each other.

"We were each getting picked on—for different reasons," Elliot said. "So we got together."

"We wanted to figure out why stuff like that happened," I said.

"No," Elliot said. "We wanted it to stop."

"Well, yeah. To figure out how we could stop it. But the things we tried at first didn't work."

"To say the least," Elliot said. "But then Catalina wrote something."

Everyone looked at her. She blushed.

"I just wrote about who I am and where I came from," she said. "Some people were saying things that weren't true. And then Mr. Dallas showed us how we could send what I'd written to everyone in school. On the network."

"On the network?" the mountain man said.

Dr. Bennett nodded. "The school has a LAN," he said. "Go on."

Catalina shrugged. She looked at Elliot.

"Then I wrote something," Elliot said. "Then other kids started writing stuff—things that happened to them. They were sending them to us, on the network. So we started *The Revealer*."

"That's what we called it," I said. "Every time we received a few stories, we would publish them for everyone—all the kids—on the network."

"Amazing," Dr. Bennett said. "Don't you think?" he said, turning around.

The mountain man and the lab lady nodded. Mrs. Capelli looked like if she moved she might crack.

"And clearly, what you did made a difference," Dr. Bennett

said. "Your survey demonstrates that. Do you think it was just because you made these things public?"

We looked at each other. Nobody said anything at first.

"We're . . . pretty sure the school atmosphere was affected," I said. "I mean, not only did the research say so, but it *seemed* that way. It just didn't seem like it was okay to do the things that were okay before. Not as okay, anyway."

I knew that was a feeble explanation. But Dr. Bennett said, "Absolutely. Because you showed people how it really is."

"We just let people tell their stories," Catalina said. "As soon as they could, they seemed to want to."

"It just happened," Elliot said. "Then when we weren't allowed to use the network anymore . . ."

"You weren't what?"

Elliot stopped. Dr. Bennett looked at each of us.

"What do you mean?"

"Well," Elliot said. "Ah . . ."

"Student access to the network was restricted," I said. "We're not allowed to use it to communicate anymore. None of the kids are."

Dr. Bennett turned around. "Why not?" he said to the principal.

"A . . . disciplinary measure," she said.

Dr. Bennett's bright eyes flicked at us, then he turned back to her. "No doubt you had to do it," he said in an understanding voice.

"Why, yes," Mrs. Capelli said. "There was some very irresponsible use of the network. There's no need to name names." She glanced at us, and smiled strangely.

"You've got a tough job to do," Dr. Bennett said to the principal in a reassuring way. "And it's not surprising that there were some problems—I mean, considering how new the network was. Still, I think you and your staff just deserve tremendous credit for opening the network to young people, and for cultivating this kind of creativity on it."

Mrs. Capelli swallowed.

"I really mean that," he said.

"Why . . . thank you."

"And I'm sure you're also teaching a valuable lesson with this suspension of privileges."

"I believe so. Yes."

"I assume it's only a suspension, of course."

"Why . . . yes. Of course."

He nodded, thoughtfully. "Did you say how long that's for?"

Mrs. Capelli paused.

"For two weeks," she said.

Dr. Bennett nodded again, his chin in his hand. He glanced back at the screen. "Two weeks of silence, to appreciate . . . communication. Why, Mrs. Capelli. How very appropriate."

The principal actually blushed.

Dr. Bennett turned back to us. "So those stories you got," he said. "They grew into this?"

"Yeah!" I said. "I mean, yes. With a lot of help."

"I see that," Dr. Bennett said. "Absolutely a remarkable piece of work. Well," he said, pushing his chair back and standing up. "I suppose we'd better pay some attention to the other exhibits, eh, fellow judges?"

But before he left, he shook each of our hands again. And I swear—Elliot and Catalina say they never saw this—but I swear he winked.

"Thanks," I said.

"Thank you."

When the judges left, Mrs. Capelli stayed. She looked at each of us. Then she sighed.

"I admit, I had my trepidations about this project," she

said. "But the judges are very impressed—and . . . well, I have to say, I can see why."

"Did you mean it about the network?" Elliot said.

"Of course I meant it. You're the ones who lost the students' access. I suppose it's only fitting that you should be the ones to win it back."

She started to go after the judges. Ms. Hogeboom and Mr. Dallas were standing there. Mrs. Capelli stopped.

"Claire, Jerry," she said, "I might thank you for bathing me in your reflected glory."

"Not us," Ms. Hogeboom insisted. "Thank them."

The principal looked back at us. She . . . nodded. Then she took off. We watched her hurry to catch up with the judges.

"Congratulations," Mr. Dallas said over his shoulder, as he went, too. "I think you won."

THE WHOLE STORY

"Sometimes I cut through here," I told Elliot, pointing up the driveway by the police department.

"Yeah? Okay," Elliot said, and we started up it.

It's funny how places that were once so deep and awful in your life can seem regular if you go there again. This was just an old driveway, full of bumps and cracks.

"You'd think the town would fix something like this," Elliot said.

"Nobody much uses it," I said. I looked across the parking lot toward Convenience Farms, where the dark shape was loitering.

"There he is."

"I see him. Is he always here?"

"Not always. But a lot."

I knew Richie would want to know. He would never come to the fair, or be seen showing an interest. But he would want to know.

"Hey," I said, when we got there.

"Hey." He nodded at Elliot. "What's goin' on?"

"Not enough!"

"So, Richie," I said. "We're pretty sure we won."

"Yeah? It went good, huh."

"It went really good. The kids pretty much thronged us. Then when the judges came, they were totally impressed."

"There's no way we won't win," Elliot said.

"You should have seen it," I said.

He snorted. "Yeah, right."

"No, really. With the judges, it was your thing that really did it."

"Yeah?" For a half second, the usual set expression on Richie's face opened up. Then it shut again.

"Yeah," I said.

"They were stunned, or something," Elliot said. "One guy said you were an incredible actor."

"He said that?"

"Yes, he did."

"This was a *judge*? What were they, morons?"

We stood there. "Didn't seem like it," Elliot said.

Richie shrugged.

"We got KidNet back," Elliot said.

Richie nodded, and looked at me. "Well," he said. "What *do* you know."

I smiled.

"So now you got something to do," he said.

"Well, yeah."

"That's good. Keep you off the streets."

Elliot laughed. I grinned. Richie even sort of, almost, smiled. He lit a cigarette. Then he seemed to think of something. He stood up from the wall and handed me the cigarette.

"Hold this," he said.

"What?"

"Just *hold* it. Geez." He opened the door and went into Convenience Farms.

I just stood there. Elliot waved the smoke away. "Phew," he said.

Richie came back out. He had a bottle of root beer.

I stood there.

With his other hand he reached out, took back the cigarette. Then he held out the root beer.

"Here," he said. "I figure I owe you one."

I took it, but I said, "I pretty much thought we were even."

He shrugged. "Then go away, all right? You want to wreck my reputation?" He shook his head. "Geez. Coupla *whiz* kids."

We had started up Union Street, Elliot and me, heading for my house. He was going to eat dinner with us, then his mom and dad and sisters were going to meet us at the Creative Science Fair. Catalina's dad was coming, too.

I took a big swig, and handed the root beer to Elliot. We passed it back and forth. When we were done I put the cap back on tight and tossed the bottle to Elliot.

He caught it and threw it back fast. Then we were throwing the plastic bottle around, laughing, tipping it up in the air, kicking it like a hackysack, throwing it off the walls of stores and catching it. We were laughing and whooping at good catches, jumping around like a couple of little kids just let out of school.

Finally we'd laughed so hard we were both bent over, hands on our knees, trying to breathe.

"What was that about, anyway?" Elliot said, nodding to the bottle in my hand. "I mean with him."

"It's a long story."

"Huh." He glanced backward, toward Convenience Farms. "You think he'll live happily ever after?"

"Who, Richie?"

"Yeah."

I shook my head. "I don't think so."

"No. Probably not."

I thought about it. "Maybe some kids are mean by nature—but I don't think he is," I said. "It's more like his life is just like that." Then I thought I might have said too much.

But Elliot was thinking. "Maybe he'll be a movie star someday," he said. "A tough guy."

"Yeah! Or maybe in jail. A tough guy."

"Yeah."

Suddenly, as we walked along, Elliot laughed.

"I don't see him writing down *his* story any time soon," he said.

"Oh, no."

"You never wrote yours, either."

I didn't answer.

"Everyone else told theirs," he said, "but you never did. I mean, what happened with him and everything."

"No."

"Why not? 'Cause it's a long story?"

"No. I kind of made a promise. To him."

"Huh," he said. "Well, why don't you write it down now? I mean, you could show it to him. It might be okay with him now. After all this."

"Hmm. I don't know."

"You could! You could tell the whole story. I've still got that first thing you wrote. Remember? That's what started this whole deal."

"I remember."

"I'll send it back to you. Then you could write it all

down—everything." He grinned at me. "It'd keep you off the streets."

I laughed. I looked at the root-beer bottle that was still in my hand. It was a little sticky.

"Maybe I'll do it," I said.

And so I did. Richie said it was okay, too. I was surprised, but he did.

And that's the whole story.

AUTHOR'S ACKNOWLEDGMENTS

Since *The Revealers* first appeared in 2003, it has been used, often in very creative and powerful ways, by middle schools, libraries, and other community organizations all over the United States and internationally. (For more on this, please see "*The Revealers* in Schools" on page 215.) When adults choose to make this novel the focal point of a reading-and-discussion project, their goal is often to open up the difficult issue of bullying. Sometimes it's just to read the book. Whatever the purpose, I am very grateful to everyone, in the hundreds of schools that have so far worked with *The Revealers*, who has played a part in any of these projects. By now you're all too numerous to even begin mentioning here by name. But thanks.

Here are my original acknowledgments for the book:

Even though all the people, the incidents, and the school portrayed in *The Revealers* are completely fictitious, I was greatly helped in developing this story by the students at three Vermont schools, who shared with me their own stories of bullying, harassment, and similar experiences. I want to thank the students, teachers, and administrators who helped me at Randolph Village School (now Randolph Elementary), Braintree Elementary School, and Barstow Memorial School, in Chittenden. . . . Thanks as well to the staff at Williston Central School, who showed me their school's local area network.

I am also grateful to the teachers at Main Street Middle School in Montpelier, Rutland Town School and Christ the King School in Rutland (all of these also in Vermont), who read drafts of this book to their classes, and to the students in those classes for their valuable suggestions and critiques. Special thanks to my friend Mike Baginski, "Mister B," an extraordinary teacher at Main Street School, for his continuing interest and support.

* * *

My journey only began with those first schools. In my years (so far) with *The Revealers*, I have done programs and joined in discussions with young people of every background, in all sorts of schools—even in a one-room schoolhouse. I've been from Maine to Florida, from Brooklyn to Silicon Valley with my book, and I'm still hoping to hear back from the teacher in South Africa who emailed that her school was reading *The Revealers* and do I ever come their way? (I replied that I'd be happy to.) I've seen how a novel can spread just because people believe in it—and I've discovered, when people do believe in a book, what champions for it they can be. Thanks to everyone, everyone, who has been a champion for *The Revealers*.

Most of all, I've seen what many adults don't realize: that an enormous number of young adolescents are avid, passionate, deeply intelligent readers. Needless to say, not every young reader I've met has liked my book, but that's not what matters.

What matters is that they *read*. I'm so grateful—and it gives me new hope for our future—to discover, over and over again, how many really do.

Finally, I'm thankful that *The Revealers* has been in some ways useful to the growing, nationwide movement to face up to bullying, to bring it into the light and help young people who struggle with it understand that they don't have to do that alone. In my travels I've come to see middle schools as laboratories for the rest of people's lives. I think what's most hopeful, and powerful, about the effort to open up new awareness around adolescent bullying is not just that some kids' burdens are being eased. It's that young adults all over the country, of all types and social situations, are getting the chance to discover that the person next to them—or on the other end of the social hierarchy—has hopes, dreams, and fears just like they do.

Early teens don't always "get" this at this stage in their lives when they're first forming their adult selves. Imagine the impact if we can help them cross this crucial bridge. I often find myself telling middle-school audiences: It's generally the kids who seem in some way different, like I was, who get singled out for bullying—but the truth is, we're all different. Every one of us is, because we're all individuals. That's the one way we're all the same.

Thank you for the chance to say that. To discover that. And to be part of this.

Doug Wilhelm
Weybridge, Vermont

DISCUSSION QUESTIONS

1. Russell is the first character to be bullied. Richie is his tormentor. How do they fit the stereotypical images of target and bully? How is Elliot bullied? How is Catalina bullied? Are the methods the same? Is there only one type of target? Is there only one type of bully?

2. Russell, Elliot, and Catalina are very different from each other. What are their strengths and weaknesses? Is there an explanation for why they're targets for bullying? Is there any justification for the bullying?

3. Richie Tucker, Burke Brown, Jon Blanchette, and Bethany DeMere are also very different from each other. Are they weak in any way? Are there any reasons for their cruelty to others? Are they good reasons?

4. Some types of bullies use their social status to torment other kids they find inferior. Are any of the bullies in this book doing that? That type of bully might be hardest for teachers to notice. Why might they be invisible to authority figures?

5. Big Chris Kuppel starts out as a supporter of Burke and Jon's behavior, but then he changes. Why? How does he treat Elliot by the end of the book?

6. Name-calling is often the first bullying behavior learned. Why is that? Make a list of the names that are used in this book to hurt someone. Are they all words that would be considered insulting if used in a different way?

7. Richie seems to take pride in being a bully, but Russell sees something vulnerable in him. Do you agree or disagree with Russell? What might be Richie's motivation? Why do you think he's willing to do the interview for The Bully Lab?

8. Do you think this book is showing something that doesn't happen very often, that bullying is uncommon? Do some research and see to see how big or small the problem of bullying is today.

9. Is bullying a problem at your school? Do you think everyone is treated equally by the teachers and principals? In the cafeteria, does everyone have a place to sit?

10. If there is bullying at your school, how does the school deal with it? Is there a bullying prevention program? Is there a way to report bullying that everyone is aware of? Do you think kids are safe to report it and that they will be taken seriously?

11. What could you do to help prevent bullying?

THE REVEALERS IN SCHOOLS

BY DOUG WILHELM

The writer of a book isn't the only person who can have a creative relationship with it. I first saw this soon after *The Revealers* was published, when a few schools in Vermont, where I live, began to work with my novel. Over the next few years, this would become something that was happening nationwide—but it started here. And in those first schools I began to see what teachers and others, including students, can do to bring a story to life.

For example, there was the morning in the South Hero "gymnatorium."

In this little K–8 school in rural South Hero, Vermont, grades 6–8 had read *The Revealers*, and they wanted to engage the younger classes with some of what the story had brought up. So on the morning of my visit, we were all brought together in the school's biggest room—the kindergarteners and first graders sitting on the floor up front, then the middle grades, then the adults, including me, perched on chairs along the sides. At this school, the upper grades had a drama club; and the drama club had an idea.

On the stage were two tables, side by side. At one sat two middle-school boys. The adult who introduced the skit said this would be based on a scene in *The Revealers*, which the older kids had just finished reading. At that point I understood: This would be the library scene, in chapter four, where Russell and Elliot watch a nasty note get dropped on the next table where Catalina, the new girl from the Philippines, has been doing homework.

But I was wrong. The situation had come from the book, but the scene was new. As the two boys watched, as we all watched, a girl came out, sat at the next table, and began quietly reading. Then out came another student, who stood behind this girl and said: *You don't belong here. You don't belong here.* She kept chanting this as another came out and said: *Nobody likes you. Nobody likes you.* And a third: *Go back where you came from!*

The younger kids, looking up, were goggly-eyed. They got it, I got it—we all got it. As the crowd behind the new girl grew, and as its cruel chanting amplified, the bullying words seemed to echo, around the room and in our heads. Everyone who was there that morning saw, heard, and felt what it's like to have taunts like these reverberate inside you, over and over, because you're different or awkward or new or you've just somehow become a target.

And I had written none of those words. Just, you could say, provided a platform.

That's what *The Revealers* has been, in school after school: a platform. The story seems to easily become a springboard for discussion, for opening up the social struggles that so often preoccupy middle schoolers, and sometimes even for breaking through to new understanding. But these outcomes don't just happen because the book is assigned or read. They are generated, I've observed, when adults—and sometimes also students—who work with this book apply their own ideas for engaging young people with it.

That is the key.

I'm very lucky. I still get to visit schools that work with my book, and often I see fresh creativity brought to the challenge of turning the story into a springboard. Sometimes I get into funny or memorable situations. I've played Alex Trebek in a "*Revealers* Jeopardy" game show that was broadcasted on a school's own TV system. I've found myself in a room full of fourth through sixth graders dressed as original superheroes, whose profiles and powers the kids had dreamed up, like the Purple Phantoms ("Our role during the reading was to find hidden acts, both good and evil"). I've listened to a classroom of sixth graders avidly explain how they put a bystander character from my story through a full-scale, court-simulation trial, where he was charged before a jury for failing to stop the bullying that he saw. (Was he convicted? From year to year, that can change.)

I'm lucky, too, because sometimes young people share things with me. At a visit I may be handed a note, often by a student who flees before I can read it. After I've been to a school, I may receive a letter or an e-mail. I'm not saying this happens every time, but it happens. "Your book relates to everybody in our school," one girl wrote. "I am not going to lie I have been bullied before, but I have bullied people before, and I am not proud of it."

I had no lesson to teach; I was trying to write a good story. What has happened with *The Revealers*, what continues to happen in schools around the country, always amazes me—and I give most of the credit to the kids and their teachers, librarians, guidance counselors, principals, and others. It takes courage to talk about this stuff in real life. And each new resonating experience always seems to have grown from someone's idea for building on the book, for helping it be the start of young people talking with each other, and hearing or seeing each other, in some new way.

One last observation. When I hear from students who've been part of a reading and discussion project with my book, they will occasionally say something like this: "I used to do that stuff," meaning bullying. "But I don't anymore."

When kids write this, they always seem to give the same reason.

The reason is this: "Now I know how it feels."

GOFISH

QUESTIONS FOR THE AUTHOR

Doug Wilhelm

Pat Hazouri

What did you want to be when you grew up?
Oh, I wanted (at different times) to be a cartoonist, a football player, an oceanographer, a rock guitarist. I had no talent in any of these areas.

When did you realize you wanted to be a writer?
I had a ninth-grade English teacher, Mr. Behr, who had us discussing the realistic novels we were reading. I had a lot to say, because I was a big reader, but I was so unpopular that normally kids wouldn't listen. Mr. Behr was tough, though, and in his class you had to listen with respect. That year, because of that class, some key turned inside me and I started writing stories and poems—even a play—but secretly, in my room. I didn't want to give other kids any new ammunition for making fun of me. But that was the first time I discovered I might have something to say, and some ability to say it. It was a turning point in my life. Thanks, Mr. Behr.

What's your most embarrassing childhood memory?
Whatever it is, I've suppressed it. I was just generally embarrassed about being me.

What's your favorite childhood memory?
When I was in second grade, we moved into a new suburban neighborhood, and I took a toy rifle and led several kids on an exploratory expedition into its backyards. The neighborhood had the typical kid-legends and rumors—that a rat the size of a cat lived under one storm-sewer grate, that some other creature of a vague sort was in the cattails somewhere else. I wanted the adventure of going to see. I remember that afternoon so clearly.

As a young person, who did you look up to most?
My parents tried, but I was raised largely by television. So my first role models were black-and-white early TV characters. The Lone Ranger. Sky King. Rob Petrie. Rocket J. Squirrel. None of these characters were actually real people, so that was, I guess, part of the problem.

What was your favorite thing about school?
Safety patrol. I got to wear a badge. Also kickball, even though I would reliably be assigned a position like "fourth right field." Only the least coordinated kids know what fourth right field is.

What was your least favorite thing about school?
Math! Also fourth right field.

What were your hobbies as a kid? What are your hobbies now?
Back then I loved baseball, the games we played in the neighborhood (we had a great neighborhood), and building airplane models. I wanted to play music, but everyone said I was terrible

at it. Today I play music! I play harmonica, conga drums, and other percussion in a band called the Avant Garde Dogs. I love it when you play and people smile, and dance.

What was your first job, and what was your "worst" job?
My first job was as a farmhand on a dairy farm in Orwell, Vermont, which is actually near where I live now. I grew up in suburban New Jersey, and in tenth grade I became obsessed with the idea of becoming a dairy farmer in Vermont. This lasted until I actually spent a summer *working* on a dairy farm. That summer I learned how to work; it was also the last time I dreamed about becoming a farmer. My worst job was doing inventory in a brass factory for a week, also as a teenager. I was horrified by the confinement of having to punch a clock, and that was the only time I ever did.

How did you celebrate publishing your first book?
I cleaned trash cans. No, I did! When the call came in that my book was being published, it was a Friday morning and I called everyone I could think of, but I couldn't reach anyone to tell them. So I left a few messages, then collected all the trash cans in the house (the little, indoor ones), put them in the bathtub, and scrubbed them. I had to do something with all that energy.

Where do you write your books?
I have written in all sorts of places, from cafés to libraries to basements to bedrooms to actual offices. I don't think it matters much where you work, as long as you work. Right now I like to write sitting on the couch in our living room, especially early in the morning. I'm here right now; I can see the bird feeder, outdoors. So can the cat.

What sparked your imagination for *The Revealers*?

My son, Brad, planted that idea. We were having lunch when he was in second grade, and he told me that at his elementary school, he and a couple of friends had a secret bully lab. I asked, "What *is* that?" And he said, very earnestly: "It's a place in the school where we lure the bullies and dissect their brains." I asked more questions and figured out that what he was really doing was sitting under a slide on the playground, during recess, and watching how some kids were cruel to other kids. Typical playground stuff. But Brad and his friends wondered: "What are those kids thinking when they do that? What's going through their minds?" That was what he really meant by dissecting brains—and that's what gave me the idea for *The Revealers*. To dissect something is to take a scientific approach to understanding it, and that's what Russell, Elliot, and Catalina try to do in the book.

Of the books you've written, which is your favorite?

I still feel partial to my first one, *The Heart of the Bazaar*, which never got published. It was a nonfiction "journey" story about traveling in the Muslim world and just talking with people. I left my newspaper job in my late 20s, back in the early 1980s, to do it. I worked on the book for ten years, and it was rejected seventy-five times. I still think it was good! But getting your first book published is very hard.

What challenges do you face in the writing process, and how do you overcome them?

The most familiar challenge is the fear. This generally comes before you start writing something. It's the voice in your head that says, "Who are you to do this? Why do you imagine this could be any good?" For me, at least, this uneasiness of fear is part of the process of doing creative work. I've learned that the more important it is for me to write something, the more challenging it is, the more scared I will feel before I start. So I just start. Once you're actually doing it, the fear will start to drift away.

Which of your characters is most like you?
In *The Revealers*, Russell began with the memory of being me—a very awkward seventh-grader (I was actually much more awkward than he is), who is bright and creative but doesn't realize that, tends to get down on himself, and is very confused by how annoyingly uncool he is to other kids.

What makes you laugh out loud?
I love to laugh! I really enjoy Jon Stewart on *The Daily Show*. I like people who make you see things in a new way—people who *see*, then find the humor that opens up the truth or helps you see, too. I'm a huge fan of humor writing, which is a very hard type of writing to do. The one thing I collect, sort of collect, is books by twentieth-century humor writers, like James Thurber and P.G. Wodehouse, who invented the butler Jeeves. He wrote over ninety novels, and I keep searching for ones I haven't read.

What do you do on a rainy day?
I might like best to go to a used-book store, poke around, then take what I've found to a café and just read.

What's your idea of fun?
I get excited to find books that you're really sorry to finish, that you keep on thinking and feeling things about. I also have fun talking with friends, telling stories, and playing music or hearing music live. My wife, Cary, and I enjoy dancing together, and we really like being on the water. If I still lived near the ocean, I would walk on the beach every day. I *love* the edge of the ocean.

What's your favorite song?

I could spend days debating that and never decide! I do know my favorite album or CD: It's *What's Going On* by Marvin Gaye. That is over forty years old, and it's absolutely about what's going on right now. Download it, you won't be sorry.

Who is your favorite fictional character?

Of all time (this one I know), it's Kim in Rudyard Kipling's 1901 novel of that name, which is my all-time favorite book. When I was in seventh grade, the age of my *Revealers* characters, my favorite was Johnny Tremain in the YA novel by that name. I would imagine myself as a minor character in that book, toasting bread and cheese late at night with Johnny in Boston in 1775. I didn't need to be a major character! A minor one was fine.

What was your favorite book when you were a kid? Do you have a favorite book now?

A breakthrough book for me in middle school—the first one that influenced me as someone interested in writing—was *The Human Comedy* by William Saroyan. This was basically a YA novel, about a poor Armenian-American boy in a California farm town during World War II who gets a job delivering telegrams because he has a bicycle. Then he has to deliver a message from the War Department, saying that a mother's son has been killed in battle. It's a fine story, but what really struck me about Saroyan's writing was its vitality. He described his approach as to "jump in the river and start swimming." Today I have lots of favorite books by YA authors—but if I had to pick a single one, I'd say Louis Sachar's *Holes*. That's just a great book.

What's your favorite TV show or movie?

Saturday Night Live. I also like the late-night comics, not just Jon Stewart but also Jimmy Fallon and Jimmy Kimmel and Craig

Ferguson. But I have to watch them on the Internet, because I can't stay up that late!

If you were stranded on a desert island, who would you want for company?
My lovely wife, Cary. But we would need someone who could find food and have survival skills—so maybe also Crocodile Dundee. Remember that movie character from the Australian Outback? But he's *fictional*. So that might not be a big help.

If you could travel anywhere in the world, where would you go and what would you do?
Twice in my twenties I spent time—once a year and a half—in Kathmandu, Nepal. That's an amazing place, and someday I want to go back. Otherwise, hmmm . . . I would like to visit Cuba, Morocco, Botswana, Kerala in southern India, and Tahiti. Give me ten minutes and I'll think of twenty more.

If you could travel in time, where would you go and what would you do?
I'd go to Paris in the 1920s, when a bunch of soon-to-be-famous writers like Hemingway and Fitzgerald were messing around, working and struggling to get noticed. I'd also like to live in San Francisco in its early boom years. I just think I would get great stories out of that place and time.

What's the best advice you have ever received about writing?
It came from an old-time newspaper man that I met when I was seventeen. He gestured toward a typewriter (this was a long time ago) and said, "Use it. Write every day." I ignored that advice for a long time, but it was very good. In a similar way, the great writer E. B. White, in *The Second Tree from the Corner*, quotes

another veteran newsman who advised him, as a young man straining for deathless phrasing on a story: "Just say the words."

Do you ever get writer's block? What do you do to get back on track?
The key for me is to say to myself, "I'm just going to write *something*. It's not supposed to be perfect; I can change it later." That takes the pressure off. If you view your first draft as a rough sketch, the way an artist sketches before painting something, then you can try stuff and make mistakes. That's the only way to free yourself to be creative—to make it safe for yourself to make mistakes, to try things that don't have to come out great.

What do you want readers to remember about your books?
I think *characters* and *stories* are what fiction is mostly about, especially YA. So I would like readers to remember my characters, the way I remember Johnny Tremain and Kim, or my stories, the way I remember *The Human Comedy*.

What would you do if you ever stopped writing?
I once taught English as a second language and loved it. I might try that again. You get to work with people from all over the world.

What do you like best about yourself?
I don't know. . . . I have a good sense of humor, and I think I am mostly kind to people. What I'm always trying to do better is *listen*. It's a rare skill, and like most people I'm not that good at it.

Do you have any strange or funny habits? Did you when you were a kid?
Oh, when I was a kid I was a whole bundle of weird nervous habits. Made strange noises, had to touch every pole on a fence

but wouldn't step on a crack in the sidewalk—I was very odd. Today, luckily, I'm somewhat less so.

What do you consider to be your greatest accomplishment?
That my son, Bradley, and stepson, Nate, are both kind, funny, hardworking, very thoughtful young men. Of course, they get most of the credit for this. But parenting is the thing that has taught me the most and has meant the most in my life. I think I write for young readers for two main reasons—because books meant so much to me when I was young, and because my boy meant so much to me when *he* was young.

What do you wish you could do better?
I believe that awareness, what the Buddhists call mindfulness—basically, just being in the present and paying attention, without judgment—is the key to living a rich, happy, creative life. So I try to be "just right here." This is like writing: You can never really master it, but it's totally worth spending a whole life trying.

What would your readers be most surprised to learn about you?
That I'm six feet ten inches tall. That's right!

You can find Doug Wilhelm on Facebook and at the-revealers.com.

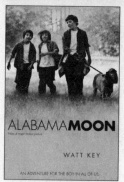